— THE BOY WITH —
FOUR NAMES

Also by Doris Rubenstein: *Itasca at 90: A history in memories; The Good Corporate Citizen: A practical guide; You're Always Welcome at the Temple of Aaron; The Journey of a Dollar; Setting the Stage: Jewish theater in the Upper Midwest from its origin to the Minnesota Jewish Theatre Company.*

THE BOY WITH FOUR NAMES

DORIS RUBENSTEIN

THE BOY WITH FOUR NAMES

iUniverse books may be ordered through booksellers or by contacting:

iUniverse
1663 Liberty Drive
Bloomington, IN 47403
www.iuniverse.com
844-349-9409

ISBN: 978-1-6632-2338-8 (sc)
ISBN: 978-1-6632-2339-5 (e)

Library of Congress Control Number: 2021910594

Print information available on the last page.

iUniverse rev. date 08/03/2021

DEDICATED TO THE COHEN-SAUER-HOCHMAN FAMILY

with love and gratitude
and gracias to the "JOEs"

PART ONE

THE BOY'S FATHER

CHAPTER ONE

A DANGEROUS SITUATION

Abraham – Abie – Cohen thought that life was pretty good in 1935. He had just graduated from the University of Stuttgart with a Master's Degree in Philosophy. He was captain of the Ju-Jitsu club there. The team had beaten every other club in Germany, Italy, and France that year. He had a beautiful girlfriend, Elsa Wagner, who didn't care that he was Jewish.

The Nuremberg Laws that Hitler's Nazi Party had passed that year changed it all.

Yom Kippur had ended the Jewish High Holidays just a week earlier. Abie had gone to the small synagogue in Aurich, in the northwest part of Germany, with his parents Jacob and Jette and his brothers and sister as they'd done as long as he could remember. His family wasn't very observant, but Abie and his brothers had become Bar Mitzvah, and Abie even had continued to study Hebrew at the University.

He just didn't see being Jewish and having a Catholic girlfriend as a problem. But the Nazis did.

In fact, even though the Nuremburg laws made their relationship illegal, he had planned to ask Elsa to marry him now that the High Holidays were past. His parents didn't know this. They didn't know that Elsa existed.

Abie invited Elsa for an early-evening walk along the banks of the boat canal that flowed through the city's main park. The canal had sidewalks on both sides and every block or two was a bridge for crossing from one side to another. Little houseboats and small barges were tied

1

up to its banks for the night and their lights and a few streetlamps were the only illumination for walkers. It was a safe place, Abie thought, to tell Elsa what was on his mind and in his heart.

"Liebchen," Abie finally said, almost whispering, "I want to ask you a difficult question."

Elsa looked at him quizzically. "I hope I can answer it," Elsa replied.

"Elsa, I want you to marry me, but first you have to make sure that you are willing to make a sacrifice for us," he said, looking seriously into her eyes. "I am a Jew and it is now against the law for us to become married in Germany. Will you leave the country with me to be my wife?"

She turned away from him. Abie was not expecting this. He expected her to throw herself into his arms with joy.

"I've got an idea!" she exclaimed, turning to him with a smile on her face. "I think it would be better if you would convert to Catholicism and change your name. If we get married outside of Germany and you change your name there, your papers would say you are a Catholic and your name would not be a Jewish name."

Abie looked at Elsa as if he were seeing her for the very first time. He stared at Elsa in disbelief.

Forgetting where they were – out in public — he shouted at her, "How can you ask me to give up being a Jew? I am a Cohen and the same blood as Moses and Aaron runs through my veins! I could *never* depart from that heritage! What you want is impossible for me!" He'd never realized how important being a Jew was to him until that moment.

In a flash, Abie realized that he had made a huge mistake. The mistake was not about falling in love with Elsa. The mistake was shouting out loud that he was a Jew.

Within seconds, a whistle blew and a policeman emerged from the shadow of a streetlamp. The policeman called to them, "Stand right where you are!"

Abie was paralyzed with fear. Elsa stood trembling. Abie knew that for him simply to walk together with an Aryan in public was against the law.

The policeman walked up to them with his baton in his right hand, swinging it slowly in a menacing way. Abie's body began to feel tense.

He felt like a screw was being wound up inside of him. Abie tried to size up the policeman as he approached. He wore the standard uniform of Aurich's police force, but he also wore a pin with a swastika on it: the man was a Nazi. He was a bit shorter than Abie, but about the same build.

"Your identification papers," the policeman demanded.

Abie stood still while Elsa searched the pockets of her coat for the little purse where she kept her identification card. It was marked with an "A" for Aryan – a "pure" German. Abie hesitated to pull out his wallet because his card was marked with "J" for "Jude" which meant he was Jewish. He was sure he would be arrested and taken to a concentration camp, if not beaten near to death on the spot!

Elsa took her time pulling out her card, her eyes shooting frightened looks at Abie all the while. The policeman took the card from her and nodded. Then he said, "Young lady, I think you may be in trouble if your friend's card doesn't have an A on it, too!"

The policeman turned to Abie and grabbed him by the arm. "Show me your card, you filthy Jew! I can see you're a Jew without it!" He tried to twist Abie's arm and pushed him toward the canal with his baton. Abie felt as if he would be pushed into the canal or have his head bashed in with the baton.

The screw that had been tightening inside Abie had become a spring and he let it loose! Everything he'd learned in Jiu-Jitsu classes came out of his body without his mind having the least control. He jumped high and kicked the policeman in the head. The man turned and fell backward hard, smashing his head on a metal pole that the canal boats used to tie their boats to the dock. The policeman was nearly unconscious, stumbling back until he fell into the river, sinking quickly.

"What's going on here?" shouted voices from boats tied up on the canal.

"Run, Abie," Elsa shouted, "Run as fast as you can!"

Abie hesitated for just one minute, to take a final look at the woman he had loved. Would he ever see her again? And then he ran!

CHAPTER TWO

ABIE ON THE RUN

He ran through crowded streets in the town square, hoping to get lost in the crowd if anyone was following him. His house, the only home he'd ever known, was the safest place he could think of at the moment.

The sound of his key in the door brought his mother to the entrance to greet him. She opened the door and looked at his disheveled clothes and his curly hair soaked with sweat. Abie could see a look of shock on her face. Every time he'd left the house recently, his mother told him to watch out for gangs of German teenagers who wandered the streets, looking for Jews to beat up.

"What happened to you, Abie?" his mother inquired, nervously. She picked up the skirt of her apron, as if to hide her shaking hands. "You look like you've seen a *dybbuk*! Did someone try to hurt you?"

Abie stopped to catch his breath before answering. "Mama, I think I killed a man. I think I killed a policeman. I didn't mean to. He tried to hurt me, tried to kill me right there on the street. I did a Jiu-Jitsu jump and kicked him in the head. I just wanted to push him away. I didn't mean to kill him."

Abie sat down on the little stool in the entrance hall. He had sat on that stool hundreds of times since he was a little boy, taking off his muddy shoes after playing soccer with his friends. Now, he sat down, covered his face with his hands and cried, "Mama, the police or the Nazis will try to find me and I will certainly be killed."

"Jacob!" Jette shouted to her husband. "Jacob, come here immediately!"

Abie's father rushed to the hallway. Abie was ashamed to let his father see him this way, sobbing like a little child. Abie tried always to be manly and athletic in his father's eyes. This is not how Abie wanted his father to see him.

"What happened?" Jacob demanded of his son.

Abie repeated his story. He didn't tell about Elsa and why he was out walking at night. He just wanted someone to tell him what to do next. He wanted them to tell him quickly before the Nazis would be able to find him.

"You must run to Holland," Jacob said calmly and without hesitation. "My cousin Albrecht is in Groningen. You remember him? We went for his son's bar mitzvah a few years ago."

Abie nodded his head.

"You must memorize his address and go to his house and tell him what happened," Jacob continued.

Abie nodded his head again.

"You will take a taxi to the train station in Emden. They'll be looking for you at the station here in Aurich. Then you can take the train to Groningen," Jacob advised. "You and Albrecht will figure something out from there."

"Oh, Papa," Jacob moaned. "How can I do this to you and Mama? The Nazis may come to look for *you*, too!"

Jacob turned to his son. "Don't worry about us now, Abie," he said and reached into his pocket to pull out his wallet. "Here is all the money I can give you now. The bank is certainly closed at this time of night and you cannot wait until the morning. Take all the money you have. Take only a small piece of baggage with you, as if you were going for a weekend visit with family. Go, now! Get your things. *Mach schnell!*"

Abie shared his room with his brother Josef, but Josef wasn't home. Neither was his sister Betti. He would not be able to say goodbye to them.

He didn't have time to breathe. He grabbed some underwear and socks and one shirt, his hairbrush and razor and toothbrush. He took some money in a bag in his dresser drawer. And, though he knew it was horribly dangerous, he rolled up his new diploma from the University of Stuttgart and squeezed it into one of the inside pockets of the suitcase.

Jacob and Jette stood at the bottom of the stairs. Jette had a small bag in her hand that she gave to her son. He peeked inside. There was an apple and some of his favorite cookies. He looked at her and gave her a tight embrace.

Jette told him, holding back tears, "If I could put all my love in that bag, I would do it."

Jacob held himself upright. Abie knew that inside, his father's heart was breaking.

"Albrecht lives at 22 Hague Street," Jacob told his son. "We're lucky that it's a short address to memorize!" And he gave a little laugh.

A taxi was waiting outside the door. Jacob must have gone to the main street and flagged one down while he was packing, Abie thought.

"Don't make a fuss," said Jacob to Abie. "Even the taxi driver must not suspect that you have any strange reason to go to the Emden train station instead of the one here in Aurich. Just tell him where to go and pretend to fall asleep."

And then he whispered, "May God watch over you."

Jacob and Abie shook hands. Abie walked to the curb, got in the taxi, and waved a cheery goodbye to his parents. It took all his strength to keep from crying. An hour ago, he'd been hand in hand with the woman he loved. Now, he was running for his life. It happened so fast. Would he ever see them or Aurich again?

CHAPTER THREE

TO HOLLAND AND BEYOND

Abie took his father's advice. As soon as he told the taxi driver his destination, he said, "I have a busy day tomorrow and I want to catch some sleep while we're on the road."

Abie didn't sleep. He couldn't sleep. Between repeating "22 Hague Street" over and over in his mind and reliving the events of the past couple hours, it was impossible to sleep. He worried about what Albrecht might think about him. It was a terrible thing he had done. Would Albrecht allow a killer to stay in his house?

The Emden station was much like the one at Aurich. There was a blackboard above the ticket counter that gave the schedule of departures and arrivals. How could it be? Within ten minutes, there would be a train leaving for Groningen!

He approached the ticket window; it was so late that there was no line and just a single clerk at the window, half-asleep in his chair. The clerk barely aroused himself to take Abie's money and hand him the ticket. The sleepy clerk forgot to ask for Abie's identification card.

Abie ran to the track where the train to Groningen was waiting, boarded, and grabbed a window seat. There were only two other people in the car, a married couple, it seemed.

Abie breathed a sigh of relief. He was almost on the way. Nothing had gone wrong with the plan. And then he remembered his father's last words to him, "May God watch over you." At that moment, Abie felt that, indeed, God must be watching over him.

7

The train pulled out of the station. The rhythmic clackety-clack of the wheels lulled him to sleep. He didn't awaken until just before the Dutch border when the conductor asked for his ticket. Abie handed it to him. The conductor looked at it, punched it, and walked on. He barely gave Abie a glance.

It was just after dawn when Abie arrived in Groningen. He walked to the information booth to ask how to get to 22 Hague Street. The attendant looked at him, curiously and asked in German, "Ach, are you from Germany?"

Abie didn't speak Dutch well at all. "Yes," he replied, "I'm here to visit some family."

"Well, good for you!" the attendant said, cheerfully. He pulled out a map and pointed to a spot not far from the train station. "You can walk to Hague Street from here." He drew some lines on the map. "Just follow the line and you'll be there in no time!"

Abie did as he was directed and found himself in front of a pleasant house with number 22 on the door and a mezuzah on the door frame. He heaved a sigh of relief. Then he knocked.

The door opened. What he saw nearly took his breath away: it was his younger cousin, Carl, Albrecht's son. He had not seen the boy since the bar mitzvah several years earlier when the boy barely looked to be thirteen years old. Now, standing before him was a young man, nearly his own height and bearing a strong resemblance to himself at that same age: dark, curly hair, blue eyes and square shoulders.

"Goedemorgen," Carl said in Dutch, with a voice full of surprise, "may I help you?"

Abie answered in his bad Dutch, "You must be Carl. I am your cousin Abie from Aurich. Do you remember that my family was at your bar mitzvah?"

Carl nodded his head, then turned around and shouted down a short hallway, "Papa! Come quick! Cousin Abie is here!" He turned to Abie and gestured for him to enter the house.

Albrecht Cohen came quickly from behind a swinging door, wiping his hands on a kitchen towel. Hot on his heels was his wife, Esther. They wrapped Abie in a strong and welcoming embrace. Albrecht looked at Abie and then at Carl, then back again.

"It's no question that you both are Cohens!" he laughed. Everyone laughed.

"Leave your bag here," Esther said to Abie. "Come into the dining room. We are just starting breakfast. Join us."

The group entered the small kitchen and then passed through an archway into a cozy dining room. There sat a girl about fifteen years old. It was Rebecca, Carl's sister. She, too, looked nothing like Abie remembered. In fact, she'd been such a small child at the bar mitzvah and so shy that Abie had almost forgotten about her.

"Look, Rebecca, it's our cousin Abie Cohen from Aurich," Esther said. "Give him a hug!"

Rebecca looked up at the stranger, but just offered her hand to him. "How nice to see you again, Cousin Abie," she responded. After Abie shook her hand, she continued, "What a shame that I must rush off to school right now. Tot ziens!" And off she went.

Esther looked a bit embarrassed. "Rebecca is very shy. Please excuse her. She'll warm up to you soon enough."

Abie sat down as Esther went back into the kitchen to bring him a plate of food. Albrecht took a cup from the sideboard and poured Abie a cup of coffee. It was then that Abie realized how very hungry he was!

"Let us speak in German," Albrecht suggested to his relative from Aurich. "Tell me first, Abie," Albrecht asked as Esther put a bowl of the warm oatmeal with brown sugar and cinnamon in front of her guest, "how is my cousin Jacob and the rest of your family?"

Abie tried to put on a happy face. He told his cousins how difficult life had become in Aurich for Jews ever since the Nuremburg Laws had been passed. Still in all, they had much to be grateful for: they still had their comfortable apartment, one of his brothers had married a wonderful woman, their health was good. He spoke in generalities, not giving many details, and the Cohens didn't ask too many questions.

Then, Albrecht asked him two important questions. "Then, Abie, what is the reason that brings you to Groningen? Why didn't you let us know you were coming?"

Abie stopped. He didn't want to tell the truth, but he knew that the truth was the only way he might get the help he so desperately needed.

He looked at each of them in the eyes. He had to trust them, although they were almost strangers. They were family. They were Jews.

"I am here" he started, "because I am running from the Nazis. I am a fugitive from their police because I killed one of them. I killed him in self-defense."

He went on to explain the whole awful story. He even told them about Elsa. "The policeman in the park wanted to kill me just because I was walking there with a German girl. That is nothing compared to what I did to that policeman! If I set foot in Germany, I will be dead in no time flat. Can you help me?"

The three Cohens sat in silent amazement. How could this be? They knew that Jews were in a dangerous position in Germany. They had seen many Jews traveling through Groningen, stopping to change trains there to go to many different cities and ports in Holland and Belgium. They were fleeing the oppression of the Nazis. These were people who had done nothing worse than live their lives as Jews. But Abie's story was something more.

Finally, Albrecht spoke up. "I believe you. You struck in a reflex without thinking. You didn't mean to kill him. You wanted to keep him from killing you. We will help."

Esther nodded in agreement. "Are you tired?" she asked Abie.

At that moment, Abie realized that indeed he was tired to the bone. The tension, fear, and anxiety he'd felt constantly since he left Elsa in the park – was it really less than a day since that had happened? – had his nerves on edge. Knowing that he was safely in the circle of his loving relatives, he felt that he could rest safely. He nodded.

"Carl," she said softly to her son, "take Cousin Abie up to your room with his bag and let him sleep in your bed. Then come right down with your books and you'll be off to school."

Abie picked up his bag in the front hall and followed Carl upstairs. Carl had barely closed the door behind him before Abie was asleep.

When Carl returned to the dining room, his father had a strange request for him.

"Carl," Albrecht addressed his son, seriously, "leave your identification card with me. You have your student identification card anyway, so you won't need it today."

Without his father telling him why, Carl took the government identification card that he had been issued just the week before when he turned eighteen and put it on the dining room table. He kissed his mother on her cheek and asked his parents, "Will Abie be here when I return from school?"

"Probably not," Albrecht answered.

CHAPTER FOUR

ACTS OF KINDNESS

Abie slept for hours, a dreamless, peaceful sleep. His mind, his body, his soul just felt safe and needed nothing more. He was awoken when the door opened, creaking just enough to bring him to consciousness. It was Esther.

"Oh, I'm sorry to disturb you," she said to him, almost in a whisper. "But Albrecht thinks this is a good time for you to be awake. Wash up and shave. There are fresh towels for a shower. Then, please, come to the living room."

Albrecht and Esther were sitting in the living room, reading the newspaper as if nothing unusual – like hosting a killer – was happening in their home. Albrecht saw Abie first and gestured for him to sit down on a small sofa. There was a cup and a teapot with some cookies on a little table between the chairs and the sofa.

"You slept a long time," Esther said with motherly concern in her voice. "Eat something now and there'll be more in a while."

"Dank je," Abie responded. His cousins were Dutch and he wanted to make sure he respected their customs and language. Although the oatmeal he'd eaten on arrival had been filling, he was ready for a snack. Esther's cookies were delicious. "These cookies are like the ones my mother makes!"

Esther laughed and went into the kitchen to get more.

Albrecht turned to Abie. "Abie, you cannot stay in Holland. Germany and Holland have an agreement to send any German criminals found here back to Germany. You must leave and leave quickly before the Dutch police get a message from the Germans to find you!"

Abie was stunned by this information. His moment of peace and freedom had been so short! His head was spinning and his hands started shaking so badly that he almost spilled his tea. His mind went blank. He'd been so sure that he'd be safe in Holland that he had no thoughts of what might come next for him.

Albrecht took the teacup from Abie's hands and moved over to sit next to him on the sofa. He put his arm around Abie's shoulders and gave them a strong, reassuring squeeze.

"Don't worry, Abie," he said, turning to his young cousin with a smile. "We have your next step planned for you."

Abie turned to Albrecht with a look that was both surprised and worried.

Albrecht continued, "You and Carl could be brothers, almost twins. I have Carl's national identity card right here." He pulled the small card out from his shirt pocket and put it in Abie's hand. "It's not hard to get him a new one; teenagers are always losing things!"

Abie looked at the card in amazement – with his clean-shaven face, the picture looked so much like himself – and then back to Albrecht with intense gratitude in his eyes. To think that these cousins whom he hardly knew would be willing to be take such chances to help him flee from the law!

"I cannot….I cannot…" he stuttered.

"Yes, you can, and you *must*," Albrecht broke in. "Do you think we Dutch people are unaware of what is happening to Jews in Germany under Hitler's laws? You killed to save your own life! As for our efforts here, there is a Jewish saying: When a person saves just one life, it is as if the whole world were saved! This is a *mitzvah* for us!"

He continued, "While you have been asleep, I have gone to the train station with this identification card and bought you a ticket to go to Trieste, but get off at Milan. It's a round-trip ticket, so nobody will be suspicious here or in Italy that you only have a one-way ticket. Hitler's laws are not respected there. It's a start. I hope that there will be some way for you to find a safe place to wait until Hitler is out of office and Jews can live in peace and safety again."

Abie turned to Albrecht and hugged him tightly. He hadn't hugged his own father like this when he set off from Aurich. Esther walked into the room with some fruit and Abie jumped up to hug her as well, almost sending the purple grapes tumbling onto the light-colored rug. Everyone laughed. How good it felt to Abie to laugh!

"This is more generosity than I could ever dream of!" he exclaimed. "How can I ever repay you?"

"God will see to that," Albrecht answered, with Esther nodding in agreement.

"I will never forget this kindness," Abie promised. "But, please, if you want to write to my parents that I got here safely, be careful how you say it. The German police will certainly be opening their mail when they realize that they are my parents."

"Don't worry about that," Esther told him calmly. "We will find a way."

Abie turned and climbed the stairs again to fetch his bag. There was a paper bag next to it. He peeked inside: two apples and the cookies, just like the kind his mother made. It was a comfort to carry these last familiar things with him to Milan. There was also a sealed envelope.

"Don't take me to the train station," Abie begged Albrecht and Esther. "Even though I look so much like Carl, I don't want anyone to see us together."

Albrecht and Esther stood up and walked with Abie into the entry hall. It had been less than twelve hours since Abie had walked into that hall for the first time, but now he was reluctant to leave it. Esther opened the door and gave Abie a kiss on his cheek. In the open doorway, Albrecht acted much as did Abie's father and gave him a hearty handshake.

"Ach! One last thing," Albrecht suddenly remembered. "Speak as little as possible as long as you are in Holland. Your identification card says you were born in Holland, but your accent gives you away as a German too easily!"

Everyone laughed. Then, the door was closed behind him.

Abie turned and looked at the door. Who would imagine that such kind, generous and courageous people lived on the other side? He looked up toward the top of the door and saw the mezuzah fastened next to it. He reached his hand up, touched his fingers to it softly, and brought them back to his lips for a momentary kiss. Then he turned and retraced his steps to the train station.

CHAPTER FIVE

ON TO SAFETY

Walking to the train station, Abie started dreaming up a new life for himself in Milan. When he was studying in Stuttgart, Abie had traveled to the Italian Alps numerous times before and after their Jiu-Jitsu competitions with the Italian team. What fun it had been to have such friendly opponents! Abie had kept in touch with a member of the team from Milan. His friend's name was Carlo Bottazzi. Abie sent Carlo postcards from places in Germany and France where the Stuttgart team had gone to compete. He liked to boast about his team's victories! Carlo was a year ahead of Abie in school. They'd lost touch ever since Carlo had graduated. Abie didn't know where Carlo actually lived in Italy since he had sent the postcards to the University sports office. In Milan? In a nearby village? Would Carlo be willing to help him?

He sat down on a bench at the station to await his train. He pulled the ticket out of his pocket was shocked at what he saw: The ticket didn't go directly to Milan. Of course, not! The fastest route would be through Germany. Even travelling as "Carl Cohen" would be too dangerous in Germany. This ticket would take him from Groningen to Amsterdam in Holland. Then he would change trains to go to Paris. The Paris train was express to Lyon. In Lyon, there was another train to Milan. It stopped in a couple cities in France and in Italy, but Abie would not have to change trains again.

That kind of route would make it hard for the Nazis to find him, if they were looking for him in Europe. He'd get off at Milan, as Albrecht told him, so the Nazis might keep looking for him in Trieste. How smart was that Albrecht!

Abie scrambled in his coat pocket for Albrecht's envelope. What he found amazed him: there was a lot of money in French francs and Italian liras! He counted the money and did some arithmetic in his head to figure out how much it was in Deutschmarks. He looked at the sign over the currency exchange window in the large waiting room of the Groningen train station. How much was this in American dollars? It was two hundred dollars! Two hundred – a small fortune at that time, enough to maintain a very simple life style for several months.

A voice came over the loudspeaker that his train for Amsterdam was ready for boarding. He waited until the second-class car was almost full to choose his seat. He didn't want to have anyone sitting next to him. He didn't want to speak Dutch with his German accent. The train jerked and pulled out of the station.

Alone with his thoughts, Abie thought back on the past days: Was it just luck that he'd been sent to Albrecht and Esther's house in Holland? The Aurich Cohens had other relatives in Holland, including on his mother's side of the family. Did Abie's parents know something about Albrecht and Esther that would make his journey better or safer?

How did Albrecht manage to concoct such a crazy route for him on the spur of the moment? And how many Dutch people kept over two hundred dollars-worth of francs and liras sitting around the house?

Could it have been that Albrecht and Esther were part of a network of Jews – and maybe even gentiles – who helped other Jews in danger of losing their lives to the Nazis to find safe passage to somewhere else? How would his father know of such a network? Would he know that Albrecht and Esther were a part of it? DID his father know? By helping people like Abie, Albrecht and Esther were putting their own lives at risk. Why would they do it?

These questions and more tortured Abie throughout his trip. He couldn't bear the idea that his parents might suffer because of his violent reaction to the policeman's effort to arrest him. Now, he had Albrecht and Esther's safety on his conscience. He twisted those questions around in his mind time and time again. There were so many train stops that he couldn't get any real sleep.

Just before the train was to cross into Italy, he went into the washroom and was shocked by what he saw: he had a heavy growth of beard on his face. He certainly didn't look very much like the youthful picture of Cousin Carl on the identity card! He fumbled in his bag to find the razor and, using the cold water, did away with as much as he could! He was going to be Carl Cohen, eighteen years old, if he was going to make it all the way to Milan.

CHAPTER SIX

A FRIEND IN MILAN

Abie had no passport, but the Dutch identification card with the name and image of Carl Cohen seemed to satisfy every border officer he encountered.

As the train crossed the border from France to Italy, Abie could see the Italian Alps to the north and he thought about his friend Carlo Bottazzi. What fun they'd had on those ski trips and during their Jiu-Jitsu matches! Abie thought that finding Carlo had to be his first order of business after stepping off the train in Milan.

Turin was the next-to-last stop. Abie stood by his seat and stretched. The next stop would be Milan – and a reunion with Carlo? What if Carlo couldn't be found? There *had* to be a synagogue in Milan; someone there might be able to help him. Maybe there were Jews in Milan like the Cohens in Groningen who were part of a network that helped fugitive German Jews – if such a network existed!

Abie's mind was drowning in such thoughts, so he almost missed hearing the conductor announce that the next stop was Milan. He only realized it when the rest of the passengers rushed to the exit to start their business trips there or visit family, or perhaps Milan was their home. He grabbed his small bag, walked down the three steps onto the platform, and took in a deep breath. The air was full of diesel fuel fumes, but he didn't mind; it was one step farther away from Nazi "justice."

"Find Carlo. Find Carlo," Abie repeated in his mind over and over again. He felt that if he thought it enough times, it would happen.

His mind took him back to the address where he'd always sent postcards to Carlo. It was the office of the Jiu-Jitsu Club of the University of Milan. It was in the Athletic Center. He knew that the University was quite far from the train station. This was the time to use some of his precious liras to take a taxi.

Milan was nothing like Stuttgart, and certainly nothing like Aurich, he thought as the taxi made its way through the roads and streets. The architecture was lighter with many buildings covered with stucco. Just about all of the buildings had red tile roofs. He compared them with the heavy stone structures and the dark slate roofs of Germany. The brightness of the sky and the colorful buildings lifted his spirits.

The taxi stopped right in front of a building with a sign announcing that he had arrived at the University Athletic Center. Abie gave the driver the fare and a tip and a *grazie*, grabbed his bag, and stepped onto the sidewalk.

The University of Milan was a beautiful place! The Athletic Building was on a large plaza with buildings around a manicured lawn surrounded by low hedges. All the buildings were of the same stucco construction with graceful doorway arches and beautiful decorations of plaster. It was more like a garden than a school, Abie thought. How different it was from the no-nonsense straight lines of most of the buildings where he studied in Stuttgart.

"I wonder if they need a teacher of Philosophy," Abie thought. "It would be such a pleasant place to work."

Yes, work! Abie had to get to work finding Carlo! He turned and entered the Athletic Center. There were students coming and going, some in their sport uniforms and some in their street clothes. None of them gave Abie a second look. As far as they cared, he looked like any other student carrying his gym clothes in his small bag. That was a good sign.

There was a directory on the wall that said: Club Sports, Room 218. He climbed the stairs and looked at the numbers on the doors, battling his way against the crowds of students going in the opposite direction toward class or home. There it was: 218. What would he find inside? Would anyone there be able to help him? His heart was pounding as he turned the handle and pulled it open.

The room was divided into different areas, each with a sign above it indicating which sport club should gather there: Swimming, Rowing, Soccer, Tennis – and Jiu-Jitsu! Abie quickly stepped over to the Jiu-Jitsu Club's table, pulled out a chair and sank down onto it in relief. It felt like home! Sooner or later, he thought, someone might come in and he could ask if they knew anything about Carlo. He pulled out the bag that Esther had given him – it seemed like a lifetime ago – and took out the last cookie, somewhat broken, but not in crumbs. That's how Abie felt about his life right then: somewhat broken, but pieces large enough to enjoy in small bites.

For nearly an hour, no one else entered the room. Abie figured that everyone was in class. There were some magazines lying around. He picked one up and leafed through it, but before he'd gotten to the end, he'd fallen asleep with his head on the table. He didn't know how long he'd slept before he felt a hand gently shaking his shoulder, and saying in Italian, "Wake up! It's time to close the room." Half-asleep, Abie thought the voice sounded familiar.

He lifted his head and through misty eyes looked up at the young man who was speaking to him. It sure looked like Carlo – black, wavy hair, bushy eyebrows, and the build of a Jiu-Jitsu competitor! The young man, likewise, looked at Abie with a look of shock in his eyes. This man sure looked like Abie, but … how?

For long seconds, the two friends stared at each other in disbelief; then, Abie rose from his chair and gave his friend and former opponent a strong hug. The force of habit overtook them for a moment and they separated to take starting poses for a Jiu-Jitsu match, then they relaxed and laughed. How good it felt for Abie to laugh again!

"What are you doing here?" asked Carlo, breathing heavily from all the excitement. "How did you get here? How did you know where to find me?" He was speaking quickly in Italian. It was hard for Abie to understand it all, but Abie could easily guess what his friend was saying.

Slow down," Abie begged, laughing. "It's been a long time since I've had to speak much Italian."

Then, carefully, he told Carlo, "I came by train over the past couple days from Aurich. I had no idea where I'd find you. I thought that someone connected with the Jiu-Jitsu club would know where you were, so I found my way here. I never thought that you would actually be here."

"Yes, I was just hired by the University to be the Club Sports Coordinator while I'm taking graduate school classes. It doesn't pay much, but it does pay my tuition and I still get to be involved with Jiu-Jitsu. But why are you here?"

"I must tell you that Jiu-Jitsu plays a big part in it!"

Then, slowly, because he was speaking Italian, Abie told his whole story to Carlo, leaving nothing out. He paused now and then to find Italian words that he only knew in German. He had to be completely honest with his friend who was the only person in Milan who might help him to his next step, whatever that might be.

Carlo listened carefully. His dark eyes never left Abie's face. He asked no questions. He could see how difficult this was for Abie. The story and the trip were amazing. Telling it in Italian was a struggle.

When Abie had finished, he put his head down on the table again, exhausted from the emotion and the memory of it all. Carlo finally spoke, "You struck out in self-defense. That is certain. If you stayed in Germany, you would have been killed. That is certain, too. I want to help you, but I don't know what I can do. I'm just a student and my family is simple farmers."

"I need a place for a night or two. Can you help?"

Carlo picked up Abie's bag. "Avanti! Let's go!"

Carlo lived in a boarding house about five blocks away. It was a large, old house behind a low wall enclosing a small flower garden. Abie followed Carlo to his room with a single bed, a chair, a desk, and a cabinet with drawers and a rod to hang shirts. There was a cross hanging over the bed.

Carlo motioned to Abie to put his bag on the chair. "I have to share the bathroom with three other students, but if you wash up now, there will be plenty of hot water and clean towels. I'll go downstairs and tell the landlady that I will have a guest for a couple days. She's really nice. Treats us all as if we were her sons!"

"I will pay her for whatever my meal costs!"

Carlo had told him that he didn't have much money. Abie didn't want to be a burden.

"Don't worry about it. We'll take care of that later." Carlo turned and went down the stairs to tell Signora Lucia that there would be a guest for dinner.

Carlo didn't exaggerate. Signora Lucia adopted Abie as easily as she had adopted Carlo. Abie hadn't eaten much more than apples and cookies for the past few days. Signora Lucia's dinner was simple, but delicious and filling.

"This is my friend Carl Cohen," Carlo announced to the other student boarders at the table. "Don't treat him badly! He's even better at Jiu-Jitsu than me!"

The other young men who lived in the house were too busy sharing stories with each other about their girlfriends and sports to pay much attention to Abie. They spoke so quickly in Italian that he couldn't add much to the conversation anyway.

After dinner, each of the other boarders went to his separate room to study for the next day's classes and exams. Abie and Carlo sat in the parlor, each with a glass of wine. They wanted to talk about good times together. They talked about skiing and about girlfriends. They talked about mutual friends from their Jiu-Jitsu clubs. They talked for a couple hours, avoiding the unpleasant reason that Abie ended up in Carlo's boarding house.

Finally, Carlo got up the nerve to ask, "So, Abie, what do you think is your next step? Will you ever go back to Germany? How long do you think you'll be in Italy? What do you think you can do here in the meantime?"

"I've been thinking about those things, but I don't really have a plan," Abie admitted. "Hitler can't stay in power too much longer, so I want to stay here in Italy to see how things shake out at home and my crime has been forgotten. I don't know what I can do with a degree in Philosophy, but I'll do any work to keep my head above water."

"Hmmm," Carlo turned, pacing slowly, "give me a little time to think it over, too. But you can see how cramped my room is here. We've got to find you something quickly. I don't think Signora Lucia would be happy for me to have a permanent roommate. Why don't you go upstairs and sleep in my bed for just this night. I'll sleep on this couch tonight; it won't be the first time."

"Danke schoen!" Abie was overwhelmed by his friend's generosity. As much as he felt he was imposing on Carlo, he knew he needed a good night's sleep. Who knew where he'd be tomorrow?

CHAPTER SEVEN

MORE GOOD LUCK

Even the aroma of strong Italian coffee and the voices of the boarders didn't wake Abie the next morning. When he finally awoke shortly after ten, he was surprised to find his underwear and shirts washed and folded, sitting on a clean towel when he opened the door to go to the bathroom. Carlo must have quietly collected them during the night and asked Signora Lucia to clean them! She was nowhere to be found when he went downstairs to thank her, but one place was set at the table with bread, some cheese and grapes, and a small pot of coffee.

He was alone with his thoughts. Mostly, he thought about finding work and a place to live.

Just before noon, the door opened and Carlo came in, all smiles. He announced, "I think I might have some good news for you, Abie."

Abie leaned forward to hear every word.

"I went to talk to the Chairman of the Philosophy Department at the University. I thought he might have use for you as a tutor in Philosophy or perhaps he knew of something in the German Department."

"Great idea...and then what?"

"We are already in the middle of the fall semester, but for the spring semester he'd been thinking of offering a course in German Philosophers to be taught in German. He wants to see you this afternoon!"

The two friends hugged each other with excitement! Abie could hardly believe his good fortune, and how much of his good fortune was thanks to his friend Carlo. His heart was so full of gratitude that he could barely choke out "Danke schoen! Grazie!" without breaking into tears of joy.

Just then, Signora Lucia came in the room.

"What's all this about?" It was a surprise to see two grown men hugging each other.

"Great news, Signora," Carlo answered. "It looks like Carl may have a job starting in January!"

"That is wonderful, but what will you do until January, Signor Carl? You are a nice man, but I do not have any room for you to stay here until then."

Abie explained that he had some money that could pay the rent on a simple room until then, and he would find some kind of work for his other expenses. He felt in his pocket for the ticket to Trieste. He wouldn't need it now. He could possibly get a refund. Every lira counted!

"Well, then, if you have some money, you must go to the boarding house of my cousin Cecilia Parise." She grabbed a piece of paper and a pencil and wrote a name and address on it. "Signor Carlo, if you are going back to the University, you can show Signor Carl the way." Carlo looked at the paper and nodded. "And take your bag with you, Signor Carl. I am sure that Cecilia has something available."

The two friends both grabbed some fruit from a bowl on the dining room table. Carlo waited there while Abie went to fetch his suitcase. Before he left, Abie put some liras on the table with a note to pay Signora Lucia for his breakfast and laundry. He didn't want anyone to think that he was ungrateful for what he'd been given. In five minutes, the two friends were out the door.

When they reached Signora Cecilia's house, Carlo left Abie at the gate and continued on to the University. Signora Cecilia answered the bell and looked at Abie suspiciously as he handed her Signora Lucia's note. Signora Cecilia thought that the young man looked safe enough that he wouldn't attack or rob her. She smiled as she read the note that the young man had a good recommendation from her cousin. That German accent, though, gave her second thoughts.

"Are you a Nazi?" Signora Cecilia asked, with a sneer in her voice. "I don't rent to Nazis!"

Abie laughed until he started coughing. "A Nazi? Me! No, Signora, I am a Jew!"

"Bene, bene!" She joined him in the laughter. And so the deal was sealed.

She gestured for him to come inside. In the dining room, she pulled a notebook from a cabinet to fill in a lease agreement. "And what is your full name?"

Abie hesitated for a minute. What should he write? Carl Cohen? No one would be looking for Carl Cohen. Then he thought about the name on the diploma from the University of Stuttgart, his real name. And this woman had already stated that she disliked the Nazis. He grabbed the pen and wrote proudly, "Abraham Cohen" in broad letters in black ink, and reached into his pocket for two months' rent. It took over half of what he had left from what Albrecht had given him.

He left his small bag with Signora Cecilia and headed to the University, remembering to bring his diploma from the University of Stuttgart. The neighborhood around the University had flags of many nations flying over their doors. He recognized some of the flags: the blue and white Greek flag, the British Union Jack. Others were strange to him. Three were almost the same; all had three horizontal stripes of yellow, blue and red. Another block down was a similar building, this one with an American flag and the Turkish flag. These houses were offices of consulates, official representatives of their countries. Milan was a major industrial city and business owners needed to have easy contact with foreign nations to make sure that goods and people could move easily between the various countries.

Once at the University, Abie asked a student where the Philosophy Department was and found the building that said "Arti Liberali" over the entrance. There was a directory by the door that said that the Philosophy Department was in room 318. He opened the door, gave his name to the secretary and told her that he had an appointment with the Department Chair, Professor Madonna. She looked at her calendar, knocked on Professor Madonna's door and ushered him in.

Professor Madonna was a short man with a magnificent head of white hair. He was built squarely. His smile was broad. When he and Abie shook hands, he put his other hand on Abie's shoulder. He put

Abie at ease. Abie sighed deeply and prepared to use his best Italian in this interview!

"You have arrived at a good time, Signor Cohen," Signor Madonna began. "We have had an increase of students from Germany lately. Many of them are Jewish. Hitler has not been kind to them. But they are excellent students and we are glad to have them. Nevertheless, their Italian often is not what it should be. I thought it would increase the number of students in our department if we could offer a course in German."

Abie pulled out his folded diploma from his jacket pocket. "I am qualified to teach beginning courses, if that is what you need. I can also tutor Italian students in German, if you know of any needing help, too."

"I will talk with the Chair of the Languages Department and see if he has a need for such help," Professor Madonna answered. "I feel confident now to list the course we have discussed in the catalog for next semester."

Abie gave Professor Madonna his new address so that the professor could send him a note about tutoring. The two scholars shook hands. Abie couldn't believe his good luck! He wanted to tell Carlo about it and to thank him as soon as possible. He ran to the Sports Clubs room in the Athletic Building to see if Carlo might be there, but all he could do was leave him a note and promise to see him soon.

CHAPTER EIGHT

THE SABBATH IN MILAN

It was a Friday afternoon and the sun would be setting soon. Abie was hungry but didn't want to spend any more of his precious liras than necessary until he learned if he would be tutoring. And then he realized: It's Friday night – *Erev Shabbos*! He would try to find a synagogue. Someone there would be sure to give him hospitality. It's a mitzvah to do that!

He didn't have to be afraid to ask about a synagogue here – no Hitler, no laws against being Jewish. He asked a traffic officer if he knew the location of a synagogue. The officer seemed confused, but when Abie asked a second time for the "Jewish Church," the officer smiled and handed him a map of the city. He drew a line to the Synagoga Centrale on Via della Guastalla. Abie could walk there.

The Sinagoga Centrale was a massive granite structure with high arches, as if it had been carried over brick by brick from Syria or Palestine. Abie was stunned when he entered the sanctuary: it could easily seat 2,000 people!

This Friday night, however, there were less than one hundred people – all men – gathered to welcome the Sabbath. The melodies used for the prayers were a mixture of familiar ones he knew from the Ashkenazi tradition of Germany. Abie took a seat very close to the bimah. Each time he stood up, he turned to see if anyone was looking at him. He gave a silent prayer that someone would approach him, as a stranger in the community, with an invitation to Shabbos dinner. Sure enough, when the group had finished singing the final hymn, *Yigdal*, he was surrounded by members of the congregation, each jostling to perform the mitzvah of giving hospitality to strangers.

One man seemed to be a leader and insisted that Abie join his family for the festive dinner. He was Roberto Capon, the president of the congregation. Later, Abie learned that Signor Capon was head of a union that served workers in Milan's important fashion industry. But, for the moment, he was just glad that his hunch about finding a host at the synagogue had paid off.

The two Jewish strangers walked briskly through the lamp-lit streets.

"What brings you to Milan?" Signor Capon asked his young companion. Signor Capon spoke excellent German.

"I recently graduated from the University of Stuttgart," Abie replied and continued, "but I cannot find work in Germany due to the Nuremburg Laws. I thought I'd try finding a job here." He wasn't telling the whole truth, but he wasn't telling a total lie to this kind gentleman. "I have just been offered a part-time position at the University and I thought I should give thanks to God and attend Erev Shabbos services."

"What luck!" exclaimed Signor Capon. "You are an observant lad?"

"Not so much," Abie responded, truthfully again. "But I know our traditions and I can read Hebrew very well."

They stopped walking at a wrought-iron gate in the middle of a high, white-washed wall. There was a beautiful mezuzah next to the gate. Signor Capon pulled out a large key and opened the gate. The two stepped inside. Electric lights revealed a luxurious garden and a large, three-storied house of white stucco and a red tile roof. This house told Abie that the Capon family had money and influence.

Before Signor Capon could even knock, the door was opened by an older woman in a servant's uniform. She greeted the two men warmly, like an older aunt, Abie thought.

Signor Capon responded told her, "This is Abraham and he will be joining us for dinner." He gestured for Abie to follow him.

The Capon house was even more beautiful inside than outside. There were colorful carpets on tile and marble floors. The couches and chairs in the living room were covered in silk cloth. The light from the large crystal chandelier in the dining room dazzled Abie's eyes before he could see that there was a group of people gathered at a huge carved oak buffet, sipping from delicate crystal glasses. They all rushed to embrace Signor Capon as he entered the room with his arms opened wide to receive their hugs. Everyone was shouting "Good Shabbos!" and hugging each other. It was a warm, Italian family.

"Basta, basta!" cried Signor Capon. "We Capons must not make our German guest uncomfortable. This is Abraham Cohen from Aurich who is here to find work teaching Philosophy."

"Please, call me Abie," he begged.

Signor Capon introduced his family: his wife, Debora, a delicate woman with pure white hair swept up into a high bun, held together with diamond clips; his eldest son Franco, a tall, handsome man about forty years old, his wife Marina and their two teenaged daughters; his younger son Nicola, shorter than his brother, but no less handsome with his wife Diana. Their young son and daughter both appeared too shy even to shake hands with the dinner guest.

By this time, another servant had set an extra place for Abie at the table and everyone took a seat. While everything on the table looked far more expensive than at Abie's home in Aurich, the blessings and the food were familiar: Signora Debora lit the candles, Abie was invited to sing the *Kiddush*, and the children led the family in the *HaMotzi* prayer over the two braided loaves of challah bread. There was chicken soup, two kinds of meat, and a fruit dessert. Dinner lasted a long time.

Abie told the family about his home in Aurich and about his family. No one had ever heard of such a small city. No one had studied Philosophy. The only person interested in Jiu-Jitsu was Nicola's little son, but he was too shy to ask many questions. Mostly, the family talked about each other. Abie was glad because he was still nervous and afraid that he might let his secret slip from his lips.

When dinner was over, it was time for the younger Capons to go home to get their children to bed and they offered Abie a ride to his room. Once there, Abie sat on the bed and buried his head in his hands. He wanted to cry, but he couldn't. Was it because he couldn't believe his good luck so far? Was it because he missed his family's own Friday night dinners together? Was it because he was still afraid that all of this might end with a knock on the door by a police agent from Germany?

Exhausted, he fell asleep, completely clothed with his shoes on.

PART TWO

THE BOY'S MOTHER

CHAPTER NINE

A BIG DECISION

Herta Sauer was an only child. Her parents, Max and Selma Sauer, were important business owners in their small, central Germany town of Tauhaubischelstein. Their textile mill imported wool and cotton, flax and silk from around the world and made it into thread and yarn and cloth that they sold throughout Europe.

Tauhaubischelstein looked like it was the model for fairy tales like the Pied Piper of Hamelin. Ancient brick churches with spires towered over the small, narrow houses on small, narrow streets below. The synagogue was almost as old as many of the churches: Jews had lived there since the 1200s, working as small merchants until the Enlightenment at the end of the 1700s. That was when Jews received full citizenship in many German states and the Sauer family took full advantage of this new freedom.

Max and Selma wanted to spoil Herta, but she'd have none of it! Herta had an independent streak. She didn't like having things handed to her on a silver platter. As soon as she thought she was old enough, she started helping her father in the factory. She mostly did book-keeping, but she also kept an eye on the machinery and the employees who made the products her parents sold. At home, the cook had difficulty pushing Herta out of the kitchen. She loved to knead and roll the rye bread they ate during the week and the challah the family enjoyed with their Friday night Sabbath meal.

Herta's independent nature extended to her education. Girls were often steered away from studying science and mathematics. They were discouraged from participating in sports. Not Herta! She wanted to learn about everything that the world and her schools offered. Team sports didn't appeal to her. Tennis was a game where she could challenge her opponents one-on-one, and she was good at it.

Max Sauer travelled all over Europe for his business and made many good friends as a result. But life was not all work for the Sauer family. Every August, they would leave Tauhaubischelstein for three weeks together on a farm in the north of Italy. The Fermi family farm produced grapes to make wines that were sold throughout Europe.

Giuseppe and Bianca Fermi kept three villas on their farm and rented them out to vacationers from across Europe. Everyone helped with the cultivation of the grapes, and everyone enjoyed the wine that was made from it when a case of it arrived at their doors in December for their own particular holidays.

Life was good in Tauhaubischelstein for Herta Sauer. As she prepared to finish high school in 1933, she thought that she could start working full time at the family's factory.

"Just give me a year or two in the factory!" Herta begged her parents. She thought that working there would give her a chance to travel some more across Europe with her father. She longed for adventure.

""No," they responded together, firmly. And Papa continued, "This Hitler man is no friend of the Jews. Who knows what kind of things he will try to do to us before the German people get wise and vote him out of office! You must get the most education you can *now* because you must be prepared for whatever may come."

There was no changing their minds, Herta knew. She needed to talk to someone more sympathetic to her own wishes. It took no time for her to walk down the street to the home of her best friend, Sophie Seligson. Sophie and Herta were just weeks apart in age and had lived on the same street as long as they both could remember. They went to the same school. They went to the same synagogue (there was only one in Tauhaubischelstein). There were no secrets between Sophie Seligson and Herta Sauer.

Herta knocked on the Seligson door and Sophie answered it, inviting her good friend to come in.

"My parents are being impossible!" Herta exclaimed.

"Let's go up to my room," Sophie replied. "We don't need to have *my* parents listening in to this conversation."

The two friends climbed the narrow staircase and went into Sophie's room. Herta explained her side of the disagreement. She told Sophie about what her parents said about Hitler. "They're such pessimists!" she exclaimed, with a sigh. "Tauhaubischelstein is *not* Berlin! This is a small town and the Christians here treat us Jews like family. They would never turn against us."

Sophie thought for a minute. She and Herta shared nearly everything, although they'd never really talked about Hitler and German politics. But Sophie and her family had talked about the situation around their dinner table many times. Sophie was not blind to the possibilities of the Nazis becoming nastier than they were already.

"Sorry to tell you this, Herta," Sophie began, "but I agree with your parents. My parents want me to go to university in Italy. Why don't you suggest it to your parents? We can go together!"

Herta was downcast. She knew there was no way out. Still, Sophie's suggestion made the prospect of leaving Tauhaubischelstein together for university studies in Italy a lot more attractive.

"Why don't YOUR parents talk to MY parents?" Herta suggested.

They did. The two girlfriends crossed their fingers and held their breath. And the two sets of parents agreed that their daughters should go together to the University of Milan. Max Sauer had business associates there and the Fermi farm was not far away.

"We will be together!" Herta shouted with joy to Sophie after her parents told her their decision.

High school graduation didn't seem so important any more to Herta. What was important was buying new, more grown-up clothes and saying goodbye to friends who were going to study in different cities. Herta left it to her parents to make all of the arrangements. The girls would share a room in the home of the Sciama family who owned a company that distributed fine cloth throughout Italy. Letters were sent to the provost of the University of Milan with copies of the girls' grades from high school, asking for admission. Granted!

When the Sauers took their annual summer trip to the Fermi farm, they took all of the things Herta would need for school in

Milan – including Sophie! The girls rowed on the lake and played endless games of tennis, stretching their muscles as much as they could. They knew they'd be spending most of their time at desks in the classroom or tables in the library.

Signor Giuseppe took everyone into Milan shortly before school was to start. They travelled in the truck that he used to deliver cases of wine to France and Germany. The girls travelled in the back with their suitcases and a few cases of wine as a gift for the Sciama family. The Sauer parents sat in the cabin with Signor Giuseppe.

Finally, they reached the Sciama house. It was huge. Signor Michele and Signora Rebeca were both dignified and friendly, in a way that can only be described as Italian. There was a large mezuzah at the entrance to the house that identified the inhabitants as proudly Jewish. Signor Giuseppe uncorked a bottle of white wine and everyone toasted the new students at the University of Milan.

Just before the Sauer parents were about to leave, Selma Sauer pulled her daughter aside. She wanted one last minute together with her only daughter. She was carrying a large cloth bag and reached into it to pull out a smaller one. She opened the small bag for her daughter to look inside. What Herta saw made her gasp with shock.

"Mama, it's gold coins and jewelry!" Herta had to control herself from shouting out what she saw. "Why are you showing this to me?"

"Herta, darling, this is your security. Things are changing fast in Europe. Who knows? This Mussolini is no Hitler, but he's no angel, either," her mother said. "Money may lose value, but these coins and jewels never will. Put this bag in a safe place and use what's inside only for the most important things, in emergencies."

Herta didn't want to believe her mother. She tried to give back the bag, but Selma Sauer would have none of it. "I told you to keep it and you will do what your mama says!"

There were many tears between everyone from Germany. There were many promises to write long letters often. Signor Giuseppe helped Selma and Max back into the truck and drove off to the train station for their return to Germany.

"Write often!" Selma shouted to her daughter as the truck pulled away.

"I will!" Herta shouted back, but she wasn't sure if her mother heard her voice.

Herta never showed the bag to Sophie or the Sciamas. As soon as she learned her way around town, she went and got a safe deposit box in the Banca Monte dei Paschi. She hoped she'd never have to use it before she graduated and returned to Tauhaubischelstein.

December 1, 1933
Milan

Dear Mama and Papa,

Thanks for your long and newsy letter. What a surprise to read about your hopes for us all to immigrate to America! It seemed to me that you were always so optimistic that the Nazis would lose power someday soon. If we do leave, I hope we can return. The Sauers have been in Tauhaubischelstein forever! I cannot imagine us living anywhere else. I miss our house and everything about our town.

The Sciamas have been great. They know everyone who is Jewish. Since their children are all grown with families of their own, I think they are just happy to have youngsters like Sophie and me in their house again!

I still have not had to sell any gold. The Sciamas really do not need the money we are paying for room and board, but Sophie and I insist on paying them. They treat Sophie and me almost like daughters.

It took a bit of time to get used to taking classes in Italian. I'm used to talking Italian, but it is another thing entirely to read complicated text books in that language. Sophie is taking Spanish. She is talking about entering the Diplomatic Corps when Hitler is gone and would like to go to South America.

I have a test tomorrow, so I will just close with hugs to you and Papa.

Your loving daughter, Herta

December 16, 1933
Tauhaubischelstein

Dearest Herta,

How good it was to read your last letter! I'm so glad that living at the Sciama house is working out well when you are so far away from your Mama and Papa. Yesterday was the first night of Chanukah. You must remember how we always put our menorah in the living room window and how we looked down the street and could see other menorahs in our neighbors' windows. No more. We lit the candles and put them on the kitchen table. We are afraid of Nazi teenagers coming and breaking our windows if they see a menorah. Why can't we be like the Maccabees and fight the Nazis? Do you think that God would make a similar miracle for us? The blessing says that God created miracles in the past and can do them today!

We haven't seen the Seligsons since the last time I wrote you. They were thrown out of their house. Can you imagine such heartless landlords? They left without saying goodbye. Perhaps they were ashamed or maybe they just wanted to go away quickly. When the Nazis see Jews walking down the street with lots of suitcases, sometimes they pick them up and take them who knows where?

We have made our application to the American Consulate in Munich. They told us that there is a quota of Germans allowed to enter the United States and that the number is under 30,000 per year. The line in Munich with people wearing yellow stars was at least 50 people long. That was just on the day your father was there! Can you imagine that same long line every day, not only in Munich but in Berlin, and Bonn, and Hamburg – wherever there is an American consulate? We will keep our fingers crossed. Yes, we have money, but we have no relatives in America and I know that those people get sent to the head of the line.

I want to wish you all happiness and success in the new year. Please give a happy Chanukah greeting to the Sciamas. Papa reads all your letters over and over again. He misses you and so do I.

Your loving mother, Selma

January 3, 1934
Milan

Dear Mama and Papa,

I hope that you both are well and that business is going smoothly for Papa.

Sophie is going crazy. She has not heard from her parents except for one short letter right after they left Tauhaubischelstein. Her mother wrote the letter on a train. But I thought the letter sounded as if Frau Seligson was afraid that someone would see her writing – as if she were writing in secret. Sophie is talking about going back to Germany to try to find them. I've told her to wait and they certainly will get in touch with her when they are settled. We shall see.

Classes went very well. I got the highest grades in all of them. I don't think I will take Economics again, though. I thought that I would study Business Administration to be able to work with Papa after I get my degree and expand our business. But I hated it! I think that I shall study more Philosophy or maybe Law.

The Sciamas are so generous to us. I have not had to touch a single coin from the bag in the bank. Like Mama said, it is for emergencies.

I will write again after classes start, but I will think of you often…always in my heart.

With all my love to you and Papa, Herta

January 19, 1934
Tauhaubischelstein

Dearest Herta,

Your papa and I are so happy that you have such a wonderful home in Milan with a family that certainly is generous. Please tell them how much we appreciate their hospitality. I will go with Papa the next time he has a business trip to Milan. You are right to insist on paying them rent, even though they may want to refuse you; certainly they do not need the money, but we are not paupers (yet) and it is the right thing to do.

We do not expect to hear anything about our visa status from the American consulate any time soon. In the month that has passed, our little Jewish community here has shrunk quite a bit, both from people "disappearing" and people leaving Germany because they have no hope for the future here. You know that Papa only goes to synagogue to say Kaddish for his parents and on the High Holidays, but he told me that when he went last week to say Kaddish for his mother, they barely made a minyan. That has never happened before, he said.

This is not the kind of news you want to share with Sophie, but if she insists on returning to Germany, let her know that we will always have room for her here.

Your birthday is coming up soon, and I wish that we could be there to celebrate with you. Enclosed is the recipe for the cake I always bake for your birthday. Perhaps Signora Rebeca will bake it for you – or you might try baking it yourself! This is the only gift I can send you right now, but you know I send it with all the love in the world, and your Papa joins me in congratulating you on this milestone 20th birthday!

Please tell us all about your classes and any friends you are meeting.

With great love from your mother, Selma

January 31, 1934
Milan

Dear Mama and Papa,

Thanks to you, I had a wonderful birthday. The cook at the Sciama house baked the cake from the recipe you sent and it was such a nostalgic taste of home. I thought of you with every bite!

The new semester is starting off fine. My Italian has improved enough for me to feel comfortable in the History class and, of course, in the Italian Literature class. I am taking the Introduction to English class. It much easier than I imagined. Philosophy is turning out to be my favorite subject. It is like exercise for the brain!

Sophie insists on returning to Germany and will likely leave in a week or two. I am worried about her and her family. I hope that someone in her mother's family in Stuttgart or someone in our neighborhood has some idea of where they might be. She knows that she is welcome in our house. I will send a telegram to the factory when she leaves so that you can expect her.

The Sciamas have introduced us to several young women whose parents work for them. Nerina Polli is a year ahead of me at the University and is an English major. Anna Bottini's family lives right next door to the Sciamas, so she, Sophie and I have been taking the bus together to the University. She is helping to show me around the city.

Signor Giuseppe stopped by last week to make a wine delivery in town and to check up on me. What a sweetheart!

I will keep my fingers crossed that your number will come up quickly to leave for America. With Papa's business contacts, he will be sure to get a job there quickly!

I will close with lots of hugs and kisses for you and Papa,

Your daughter, Herta

February 11, 1934
Tauhaubischelstein

Dearest Herta,

I am so glad that we were able to send you to Milan! Your life there sounds as good as it can be, considering that we are not with you. We miss you constantly.

Things are getting even harder for Jews these days. I am glad we do not live in a bigger city. I hear that Jews in bigger towns are being forced to leave their houses and live in areas that are designated as ghettos. My goodness! German Jews have not had to live in ghettos for over a hundred years – we are full citizens! Here in Tauhaubischelstein, as you know, the Jewish community is small and live pretty much in the same neighborhood anyway, so there's no need to create a ghetto. I hope it never comes to that here.

Frankly, I do not listen to the news on the radio very much. It is too depressing. My happiest thoughts are of

you and your life in Milan. Don't get too happy there, or you may not want to leave it to join us in America!

I am leaving this part of my letter for the last. We received your telegram about Sophie about five days ago. She still has not arrived. I am just hoping that she went to Stuttgart to see her relatives there and just failed to inform us. Unfortunately, I don't know how to contact her there. Let's keep our fingers crossed that she will show up soon.

Please give my warmest regards to the Sciamas and to the Fermis the next time you see them.

Papa asks me to tell you he sends giant hugs! We love you so much.

Your loving mother, Selma

March 1, 1934
Milan

My dear, dear Mama,

I am so glad that I have good news to share with you and Papa since so much of what you tell me about the events in Tauhaubischelstein is not happy at all. Thank you so much for all you have done for me to keep me safe and continuing my education. I love you.

All of my classes are going well. I struggle a bit with English. The teacher wants us to speak with American accents and I have a lot of trouble pronouncing the "r" correctly! If that's my worst problem, then I am truly lucky! I especially enjoy my Philosophy classes.

I am disturbed that I have not heard from Sophie, either. She promised to write when she arrived at our home with you and Papa. The more bad news you send me, the more my mind fills with fear for her. She is like a sister to me, you know. Where can these people be going? Why can't they write to their families and friends? Please send a telegram if and when she arrives and I shall do the same for you if she returns to Milan.

On Sunday, the Sciamas and I drove out to the Fermi farm for a day. Spring comes a bit earlier here than it does in Tauhaubischelstein and the first leaves are starting to sprout on the grape vines. They were very impressed with "our family's" little villa and the tennis court. How I wish you had been with us! Maybe, someday soon?

I miss you and Papa so much and send you all my love.

Your daughter, Herta

April 14, 1934
Tauhaubischelstein

Dearest Herta,

Please forgive the tardiness of this letter. There has been so much going on in Tauhaubischelstein and around the country that I did not want to put pen to paper; it would make it all too real. Whatever news about Hitler that you read in the newspapers or hear on the radio is true and probably worse than what they are telling. He and Italy's Mussolini are getting quite cozy, it seems, and that does not bode well for the Jews of Italy.

The good news is that we had a lovely Passover. It was very difficult to get matzos and other kosher for Passover foods, so we ended up having a community seder at the synagogue. The hazzan led the ceremonies and it was so enjoyable to hear him chant everything in his beautiful voice. I helped in the kitchen a bit. I was sad, though, that I was not able to prepare some of our family's favorite dishes like the matzo kugel that you like so much. The congregation is dwindling. People are leaving every week – people like us whose families have

*been in Tauhaubischelstein for generations. Enough! I
will get sad.*

*The good news is that your Papa and I are in excellent
health. We remain hopeful that we will get a visa to go to
the United States before the end of the year. The Frenkel
and the Jonas families both left for Chicago just before
Passover. There is hope!*

*On that happy note, I shall put all of my love into this
letter, along with your Papa's hugs.*

Your loving mother, Selma

May 2, 1934
Milan

Dear Mama and Papa,

*I enjoyed reading about your Passover seder. I wish
you'd have sent your matzo kugel recipe; I missed it at our
seder. I miss so many things about Tauhaubischelstein, but
mostly I miss you two.*

*I am writing this letter just before I sit down to write
my final papers and take my final examinations for the
semester. I hope that I will do well for your sakes as much as
my own. I know that I will not have time to write again
until they're all over.*

*You are right that Mussolini is no friend to the Jews.
The Sciamas usually have a couple dozen guests at their
table. This year it was just Signor and Signora Sciama,
our neighbors, and me. Just as in Germany, many Jews
are leaving Italy. And just as in Germany, the Americans
are making it very difficult for them to get a visa without
relatives living there already. It seems that many are going
to places like Cuba. Any port in a storm, I suppose!*

*The Fermis have asked me to come back to the vineyard
to work and stay with them during the summer. I told them*

that I would love to do it. I won't earn much money, but it will remind me of our many summers there together. I know they will appreciate my help. Signor Giuseppe told me that he has not gotten a single reservation to rent a villa from any of his longtime German guests and his income from families like ours in Germany is down to nothing!

So, please be patient and I will write with information about my grades after exams.

Hugs and kisses from your daughter, Herta

P.S. No news from Sophie.

May 30, 1934
Milan

Dearest Mama and Papa,

Just because I told you that I would not be writing you for a while is no excuse for you not to write to me! Please answer this letter quickly and tell me that all is well with you in Tauhaubischelstein.

First of all, I must tell you that I think you will be proud of my academic progress here in Milan: I received a 100% in Philosophy, 100% in both American History and Italian Literature, and 88% in English (it's that accent that brought my grade down, I'm sure!). I am already registered for my classes in the fall: Advanced Beginning English, Italian Philosophers of the 16th Century, Italian History, and a seminar class in Philosophy where I will have to create a lesson or two for my classmates. I hope that I have as much success in these classes as I did already. Please don't feel nervous about all my classes relating to Italy. I have every intention of returning to Germany when I graduate.

Please send your next letter to the Fermi farm. They will be glad to see a letter from you in their mailbox! Think back on our happy times there together.

With all my love to you and Papa,
Your daughter Herta

CHAPTER TEN

1935 AND 1936

As the years went by, although Herta and Selma had promised to write each other often, the time between letters slowly became longer and longer. Herta had created a new life, an exciting life of learning. The Sciamas and Fermis were like second parents to her, and she missed her parents in Germany less and less. No one heard from Sophie, ever.

The letters that Herta received from her mother became increasingly sad and worrisome. They made Herta sad and upset.

Life under the Nazis became more restrictive and threatening for Herta's parents. Her mother's hope for approval to flee to America seemed an impossible dream. Selma was on a carousel, it seemed, reaching out for the brass ring that would give her another ride – another life – was always just beyond her grasp.

Max's business was faltering. Many of his customers and suppliers were Jewish and it was becoming more and more difficult to deal with them. Since the Nuremberg Laws were being enforced more strictly in larger cities, a lot of Jewish businesses had been forced to sell to the Nazis or close. That hadn't happened yet in a small town like Tauhaubischelstein, but Max dreaded the day that he knew was coming and he would no longer have a source of income. He hoped the Nazi nightmare would end and that they could get back to life as it had been before.

The school year that started in the fall of 1935 was different for Herta. She had to decide on a major. She still thought about Business, but felt that she knew more than some of her professors. Her father had been a good teacher, at least when it came to *his* business. She thought Law might be good. But the laws in Italy were different than German laws. And the German laws were getting worse and worse by the day for Jews. No, it wouldn't be Law. It would be Philosophy.

She dived into it and looked forward to graduation.

January 30, 1936
Milan

Dearest Mama and Papa,

> *I am so glad that this will be my last year away from you. Yesterday was my first day of classes for my last semester and I have a demanding schedule, so I want to write to you before I get too busy.*

> *What I look forward to the most is writing my Senior Thesis. I want to write about German Philosophers of the 18th Century. It's my luck that there is a new instructor in that very subject. I'm sure he is Jewish, Abraham Cohen. I think he's from Aurich. The class is in German, so it will make my thesis much easier since I won't have to read the texts in Italian and then re-translate them back into German. The Dean says that I can write the thesis in German, too!*

> *I am sad that you will not be coming to Milan on business this year again. Yes, it must be frightening to think that if Papa leaves Tauhaubischelstein for more than a day that the Nazis will try to seize the business. I went to synagogue with the Sciamas during Chanukah for a special program. I could not help but notice that several families who are pillars of the congregation were not there. Jews are leaving Italy in great numbers. When will the world come to its senses?*

> *I hope that my letters bring you some cheer. You were so wise to insist that I leave Germany for my university*

studies. I cannot thank you enough. You and Papa are the best parents ever!

With all the love in the world from your daughter
Herta

Abie and Herta worked together closely as teacher and student that semester. Abie was impressed with the sharp mind of his attractive student. She was so different than Eva, and that was a good thing. He knew he had to forget Eva, forget why he had to leave Germany. But Herta was more than a distraction from painful memories. He felt himself falling in love with her. How did Herta feel?

May 13, 1936
Milan

Dear Mama and Papa,

I was heartbroken that you could not be here for my graduation. Both the Sciamas and the Fermis were at the University for the ceremony in loco parentis, but they could never take your place. Enclosed is a photo of me in my cap and gown with them. The other person in the photo is Abraham Cohen, my thesis advisor, and now my good friend.

I am also disturbed that you do not want me to return to Germany. I really do not want to wait here until you have emigrated to America so I can join you there. You have been waiting for years already to get a visa to go there and nothing has happened. I understand that you do not want to sell the business until you are leaving for America for good. But I have spent practically nothing from my little sack of gold. Can't we use this to live together in Italy? Perhaps Signor Michele will employ you in his business!

Enough of my nagging! You have been wise in all your decisions so far. Even though I now have a degree in

*Philosophy, I don't think it qualifies me to tell you how to
live your lives. Please be safe and know that I love you both.*

Your loving daughter
Herta

Indeed, now that Herta was no longer Abie's student, he could start
acting like a boyfriend, even a suitor. He thought that Herta was the
kind of woman he should marry. He only hoped she felt the same way
about him.

Would she feel the same way once she knew his secret? Should he
tell it to her? It was better to tell the truth sooner than later.

June 8, 1936
Milan

Dear Mama and Papi,

*There is something on my mind that I must share with
you. The truth is that my feelings for Abraham Cohen,
my former professor, have always been more than just
the admiration of a student for her teacher. Things have
progressed quickly since graduation at the end of April. We
both realized that there is something special between us.*

*I must tell you that shortly after my last letter, Abie
made a startling confession to me. He told me why he came
to Italy. It was not because he was seeking work. When he
was in Aurich, he killed a Nazi police officer and had to flee
Germany. He described the entire incident to me and I have
no reason to think that he was telling me anything but the
truth. It is clear that he did not intend to kill the officer and
that he was acting in self-defense. I believe him completely.
He seemed so relieved to be telling me the story. It's as if he
hadn't told anyone else and that the stress of hiding the truth
was causing him all kinds of nightmares. He now has terrible*

guilt that it is his fault that his family has disappeared and may well be dead at the hands of the Nazis.

Our relationship is becoming serious and I didn't want to hide anything about him from you. Please do not think that he is a bad person. He is not and I respect him a great deal. I think I love him, and you will love him too, when you meet him. I only hope that we all will be together soon.

With love and hugs,
Herta

Even so, with school over, Herta left to spend the summer at the Fermi farm. She had become so experienced in the operations of the vineyard that they refused to take any money from her. Herta was happy about that. Since money was tight for her parents at home, she had only had to sell one gold necklace to pay for the last semester at the University and her room and board with the Sciamas.

Herta knew that Abie had very little money. She always suggested that they go to free programs and events at the University. She didn't want to embarrass him if he couldn't pay for her at movies or anywhere else with an entrance fee.

Abie missed Herta badly during the summer of 1936. She seldom came into Milan and he had no way to get out to the country. No trains or buses went close to the Fermi farm. When she came back at summer's end, Abie knew exactly what he wanted to say to her.

It was just before Rosh HaShana, the Jewish New Year. Abie hoped to be invited to the Sciama house to share in the holiday meal if Herta were there. She was.

He sat with Herta in the garden of the Sciama house, waiting to be called in to join the family for dinner. Now was the time!

"Meine liebe Herta," he said to her in German, the language they both felt most comfortable speaking, even after a year in Italy. "All this summer, I was desperate to see you and talk with you."

Herta nodded. She'd missed him, too.

"You know me better than anyone else. You know the good and the bad – and very few people know the bad."

She nodded again. Either he was going to propose or he was going to tell her that he was leaving Italy. She put her hand in his.

"We don't know what awaits us here in Italy. Every day, Mussolini's words and actions frighten me more and more. I don't know if I have the strength to run again if he and Hitler agree to start looking for me. But I know I'll have the strength if you are by my side as my wife." Abie looked deeply into Herta's eyes. "Will you marry me?"

"I do want to marry you, Abie," she replied, "but I am nervous about doing it without the blessing of my parents. Even though I've told them about you and they have not objected to us dating, I know they couldn't come to Italy for a wedding and I can't imagine doing it without them here!"

Abie threw his arms around her and kissed her with all the energy he could muster. "But you DO want to marry me!" he cried. "We will find a way!"

"Let's announce it to the Sciamas at dinner!" Herta replied with joy. "What a wonderful way to start a new year!"

The Sciama's housemaid opened the door to the garden just then. She was embarrassed to see the young couple in each other's arms.

"Dinner is ready!" she announced, and turned away quickly, with a little giggle.

The Sciama home was a happy place always, but when Herta and Abie made their announcement, the happiness seemed to shine everywhere: in the candles as they were lit and blessed, in the glasses with wine as they were lifted for Kiddush.

"May Herta and Abie's love always be as sweet as the apples and honey that are a part of our new year's celebration!" Signor Michele declared, and offering a slice of apple with honey to his wife, he added, "May your life together be as happy as ours!"

That very night, Herta wrote a letter to her parents in Tauhaubischelstein. She hadn't written to them during her whole summer at the Fermi farm.

September 19, 1936
Milan

Dearest Mama and Papa,

First of all, I want to wish you a Shana Tovah! My most fervent prayer is that we will be reunited at last during this year.

Please forgive me for not writing more often. I have no excuse. But now I have a wonderful reason to talk to you in this letter. I have told you about Abraham Cohen and all that he means to me. Tonight, on the eve of this holy season, he asked me to be his wife and I told him yes – but it would not be final until I received your blessing. And I would not want to be married without you and Papa to walk with me and stand beside me under the chuppah.

I must tell you that the whole Sciama family is thrilled with this news. They see how hard Abie works and how modestly he lives. I hope that perhaps Signor Michele will offer him some sort of job with his company so that he can earn a good living. But there's a lot of difference between being a philosophy professor and a business man!

Do you think there is any way that you could come to Milan for a wedding? You can imagine that it is far too dangerous for Abie to return to Germany for us to be married there. We have not set a date, but I'd love for us to be married on the first day of Chanukah, especially since we have become engaged on a Jewish holiday. Please make this impossible dream come true for me!

Please, Mama and Papa, tell me that you give Abie and me your permission and blessing to marry. And please tell me that you will be by my side under the chuppah.

Your loving daughter, Herta

P.S. I can sell another piece of jewelry to cover the costs of your travel and the wedding.

September 29, 1936
Tauhaubischelstein

Dear Herta,

A happy new year to you, too! The news of your engagement was not a big surprise for your Papa and me. The way you have described Abie makes us confident that he will be a good Jewish husband for you. We are glad that the Sciamas also approve of the match. We know that you and he truly love each other and that you will have a good life together.

Papa and I are very sad to say that we want you to go on with your wedding plans in Milan without us. Do not delay the wedding because of us. My heart is breaking as I write this. I feel so selfish to tell you that we do not want to endanger our immigration to America with even a short trip outside of Germany. We will celebrate your marriage a second time when we are back together some time soon!

I must also tell you that Rabbi Siegel has disappeared, so he couldn't perform your wedding here even if Abie could come to Tauhaubischelstein. My prayer is that he fled and was smuggled out of Germany and is not in some Nazi prison for no reason at all other than he is a Jew and a rabbi. It was a very small group that gathered at our shul for the High Holidays. There were only twelve men, so at least there was a minyan to read the Torah.

Papa's business is falling apart. His non-Jewish customers are being pressured not to do business with him. To think that people who have been our long-time customers are turning their backs on us is as sad as it is painful for the loss of business.

Please, my dear, whenever you have the wedding, take a picture or two so that we can see how beautiful you look and to see the happiness on your face and on Abie's.

Please give our regards and thanks to the Sciamas and the Fermis. And, of course, please give your fiancé a big hug from your Papa and me. We are already calling him our "son."

With all my love, your Mama Selma

CHAPTER ELEVEN

A YEAR OF CHANGES

So it was done and decided. Herta's parents had given their permission and their blessing. Herta's heart was bursting with both joy at the prospect of marrying a man she truly loved, and with sadness that her loving parents, who had sacrificed having their only daughter with them for her own sake and safety, would not be with her for the most important event of her life.

The wedding would be small, the happy couple, agreed. To save money, they decided to use a gold ring that was among the jewelry Herta had brought from Germany as the wedding band. The ceremony would be in the rabbi's study at the. Sinagoga Centrale. The Sciamas would stand with Herta, in place of her parents. Abie made one special request: He wanted his friend Carlo Bottazzi, a Catholic, to be his best man. Who could say no to that?

Herta had no time to plan for a reception. She had finally finished her education and was proud of her accomplishment. What she'd do with it was another question! Her parents had sent her to Italy to get a degree and that's what she did without their help or interference.

On the first night of Chanukah in 1936, Herta Sauer and Abraham Cohen stood together with people who had come to be like family to them, in the rabbi's study of the Sinagoga Centrale. Michele Sciama, held one of the poles supporting the chuppah. Giuseppe Fermi, who had known the bride since her early childhood, held another. Carlo Bottazzi held the third. The two Catholics looked a bit confused over these unfamiliar rituals and strange language. Roberto Capon held the fourth. Rebeca Sciama held a picture of the bride's parents. Bianca Fermi held the bride's flowers when it was time for Herta to receive her ring.

At the end of the ceremony, Abie stamped on a small glass goblet wrapped in a napkin and everyone shouted "Mazel tov!" when the newlyweds kissed. They all went to the Sciama house for cake – Herta's favorite-- baked by the Sciama family cook, and some wine provided by the Fermis.

Herta had packed up her belongings to take to her new home. When the last member of the wedding party – Carlo Bottazzi – left the house, Signor Michele put the suitcases and boxes into his car and drove the happy couple to the small apartment that Abie had found to be their first home. There was no honeymoon. Classes would start in a couple weeks and Abie had work to do to prepare. Herta did a little office work for Signor Michele.

February 18, 1937
Milan

Dearest Mama and Papa,

You must be surprised to receive another letter from me so soon after my last one, but I must share this wonderful news with you: You are going to be grandparents! I had the test done last week and we just got the results today. The baby is due in September. How I hope we will be together for the birth. You could not be at the wedding and I cannot bear the thought of you, Mama, not being here with me to welcome your first grandchild into the world.

Mama, please tell me that you and Papa will be leaving Germany soon. You have made so many sacrifices for me. I can't bear to think that you won't be able to meet your grandchild when he or she is born so that you can be one of the first to give a first embrace. Please write soon. Abie joins me in all of these wishes.

Your most loving daughter, Herta

February 27, 1938
Tauhaubischelstein

Dearest Herta and Abie,

Your last letters have been such a blessing to Papa and me. There is a special place in heaven for people like the Fermis! How well I remember the warm summer nights when we sat out on the villa's patio, nibbling on the first ripe grapes and having contests of who could spit the seeds the farthest! Papa and I are so glad that we insisted on sending you to finish your studies in Italy. You have found love and a safe refuge there.

The news of the arrival of your child in September makes us happier than you could ever imagine. It is the only happy news we have heard from anywhere lately. We received a very sad letter yesterday from the American Embassy in Berlin. We have been denied entry into the United States and there is no chance for us to re-apply or ask for reconsideration. We have had all of our hopes tied to the United States and have not made applications to any other country. I know that there are long waiting lists to go to Canada, Australia, and even Argentina where many of our friends and business associates have gone. We feel so alone.

The Nazis are trying to take over our business. There is no one else in Tauhaubischelstein who knows every part of the textile business like your papa, so they are allowing us to stay. But they want us to start production on different kinds of cloth than we have produced before, particularly heavy canvas, like the kind used for camping tents. Papa has to make many adjustments to the machinery, and he is taking his time about it just so that he will have work to do. Any Jew without work somehow disappears off the streets in a short time. Anyway, the Nazis provide the raw materials. They pay for Papa's work on the factory

*floor and me in the office very little. I have taken all of
our money out of the bank and have it hidden around the
house. I don't trust the Nazis enough to think it would be
beneath them to raid the bank accounts of Jews!*

*Papa and I read your letters over and over. They
make me happy in these times of fear and uncertainty.
Knowing about this baby and that you and Abie are
happy is the best medicine for my sad heart.*

With all love from your mother, Selma Sauer

"We're going to need a larger place once the baby arrives," Abie told
Herta one late afternoon. Even so, he knew her well enough to know
that she had been thinking of this already. "And we've got to find a place
to stay that is even cheaper than this little apartment."

"What do we do? Who will rent to a Jewish family now at *any*
price?" Herta asked her husband, downheartedly. "We thought we were
safe and even welcome in Italy! We can't go back to Germany!"

Their whole world had just turned against them, they thought.
Shortly before the end of the school year in 1936, the Italian dictator
Mussolini decided that he liked what Adolf Hitler was doing in
Germany. He announced that Jews could no longer teach in universities,
that Jewish children could not attend Italian public schools.

The young Cohens were devastated. Abie's job certainly would
end before the baby's arrival. Herta felt that she wasn't really needed in
the Sciama's office. It was like taking charity. It was a blow to a young
couple who were educated, physically fit, and willing to do whatever it
took to make a good life for the child they wanted to welcome into a
happy, secure home.

"We need a place to look at our options, even if it's temporary," Abie
suggested. "How I like it here, though."

Herta went into the tiny kitchen to fix some tea. She needed a few
quiet minutes to think.

When she came back with a tray of tea and cookies, she said quietly,
"We might go to live with the Fermis at the vineyard. We know that

they had almost no customers coming from Germany last summer. The villas will be empty."

Abie barked back at her, "Do you mean take charity from them? They have been so good to you already! I will not beg!"

"No, no," Herta replied, patting his arm. "We will work on the farm. Whatever work needs to be done, we will do and we will not take money from them. I will sell another necklace or perhaps one of the brooches – the one with emeralds should bring a good price! We can pay for our food that way."

Abie looked at his young wife with love. She was so practical! He was a dreamer.

"Get out some paper," he told her, "and let's write a letter right now to the Fermis. It can't hurt!"

Herta wrote:

June 6, 1937
Milan

Dear Signor Giuseppe and Signora Bianca,

It was wonderful to have you with us on our wedding day. How many things have changed in such a short time. I must punish myself that I have not told you sooner, but Abie and I are expecting a baby in September!

We are certain that you have read in the newspaper or heard on the radio that Mussolini has forbidden Jews to teach at any level in Italy now. This is terrible news for us. Abie has been quite successful and popular with his students at the University of Milan. We thought that he would continue working there for the foreseeable future.

Now that future has arrived and it is not what we thought it would be. There is no hope for either of us to work in education in Italy and we cannot return to Germany. We need a place to stay until we can figure out what and where we might make a life together. We are asking you to once again extend your generosity to me and now to Abie and

63

allow us to live in one of your villas – and work for you as payment for rent. We will never be a burden to you!

Please answer this letter as quickly as possible. Our rent is paid for June, but we need to make a change as soon as possible. We will accept whatever decision you make with no bad feelings toward you if you say no.

With all warm regards, Herta and Abie Cohen

The next day, Herta mailed the letter at the mail post office in Milan. Then, she went to the Banca Monte dei Paschi and withdrew the gold and emerald brooch. She went directly to a jewelry store owned by a member of the Sinagoga Centrale, Signor Finzi, and sold it. The owner could easily guess why such a young, Jewish pregnant woman was selling it and gave her a good price. She went back to the bank and deposited most of it in her account. The amount in her bank book had been getting smaller and smaller over the past months, and it felt good to see the total climb to a comfortable level. This all was her money, even though she and Abie were married. The money and the jewelry had come from her parents and she wanted to watch over it by herself.

Before she left, she stopped and asked the teller, "Does Banca Monte dei Paschi change money? Can I take some of my liras and change them into Deutschmarks or English pounds or even American dollars?"

"Why yes, signora," the teller replied. "We charge a small fee to do it. We can also make money transfers by wire to many major banks in Europe. That costs less and is safer than sending money to another country by mail."

Herta hadn't thought of that possibility. It was good to know. Such information might be useful one day. She folded the money and put it in her purse. It should last for a few months, if nothing awful happened.

Nothing awful happened. A week later, in the early the morning, the Fermis knocked on the door of the Cohen's apartment. The Cohens were home to open it.

"Hurry, hurry!" Signor Giuseppe shouted, still standing on the doorstep. "We are here to help you pack your things and take you to the farm! There's work to be done there! Look! Our truck is right here, with the engine running!"

Abie turned to his wife and said, "We wrote to the Fermis to rescue us. Here they are, knocking on our door to take us to safety. We just need to stop at the Sciama house let them know you will not be working for them anymore." Turning to the Fermis, he said, "Come in. We have few belongings; this is a furnished apartment."

The Fermis looked at Herta. "And this," Signora Bianca said, pointing to Herta's stomach, "is the most important reason for you to be with us!"

Everyone laughed and hugged.

Within an hour, the suitcases were packed. Abie went to the basement office of the building manager and handed in his keys. The manager looked at him curiously. This young couple had just moved in! Why would they leave so soon and so suddenly? He just asked where he should forward any mail. Abie gave him the address of the Fermi farm, a sincere "grazie," and headed back to what had been his home for those few months. The truck was loaded. Abie kissed Herta, took her hand and helped her into the truck. This was not what he had hoped for, but he still was safe.

"Buona fortuna!" the Sciamas said in one voice when the Cohens knocked on their door with the news of their move to the country. "Keep us in touch! We want to know when il bambino arrives!"

The Fermis had not exaggerated. There was a lot of work to be done in the fields. There was work in the building where there were vats to ferment and age the wine, and the bottles, the crates. The wagons used to carry tools needed to be repaired. Abie enjoyed driving the wagons. He liked the horses and they liked him. Both Abie and Herta did all the work that both of the Fermis did.

As agreed, the Fermis did not give the young couple salaries. The Cohens received no money, although they did receive a weekly bottle of wine for free. But the Fermis charged no rent for the little villa that Herta had called her summer home for many years. The young couple stretched every lira to make ends meet. Herta didn't have to go into Milan to sell more jewelry to keep them going.

Herta wrote to her parents:

July 1, 1937
Fermi Farm, Puegnano, Brescia, Italy

My dearest Mama and Papa,

Where has the time gone? I feel terrible that I have not been writing frequently, as I promised you when I left Tauhaubischelstein. But then, again, your letters have been few and far between as well! The last note I got from you was short and with no news other than things were getting worse.

You can see that Abie and I are back at the Fermi farm. The move here has been a blessing. Since neither Abie nor I can find professional work in most places in Italy ever since Mussolini's horrid announcement, being at the farm is peaceful work and keeps our minds off of what was starting to scare us in Milan. The villa is just like it was when we came here as a family. Sometimes I think I see you sitting on the patio when the sun is going down. Now Abie is my family and he loves sitting on the patio when the sun is shining from the south.

We work very hard on the farm. The neighboring farmers know that the Fermis have lost all of their German visitors who helped with the vines in the summer. They tried to take advantage of the Fermis' sad situation by charging lots of money to help with the harvest. Now, with Abie and me here, the neighbors are not needed. So, both the Fermis and the Cohens are benefiting from this arrangement.

I believe that this work is making me strong. I hope that I will be very strong when it comes time to deliver our baby. Mama, I so want you to be here. And if it is a boy, it would be wonderful for Papa to welcome a grandson into the Jewish covenant with God.

In the evenings, Abie and I spend much of our time reading poetry and philosophy to each other. Our favorite is Heinrich Heine. You know there is no electricity in the villa, so we read with a kerosene lantern or by the fireplace — how romantic!

Abie's dear friend Carlo Bottazzi has visited a couple times. The two of them are like little boys when they are together, practicing Jiu-Jitsu! He is such a pleasant person and has been a loyal friend to Abie. I am quite fond of him.

If things get worse at the factory, please try to find a way to come here. Abie is looking forward to meeting you when we are reunited! He and the Fermis join me in sending our love,

Your loving daughter, Herta Cohen

PART THREE

A FAMILY IS FORMED

CHAPTER TWELVE

THE BOY GETS HIS FIRST NAME

It was early September and the grapes on the vine were bursting with juice. Sometimes, Herta laughed to compare her growing stomach with the ripening grapes: both were round and firm. Signora Bianca made her do exercises to prepare for the birth. She was a midwife and could deliver the baby right there in the villa. The exercises helped, but as her due date grew closer, Herta's stomach was too big for her to stand on her feet and harvest the grapes, but she worked seated inside, preparing bottles.

Herta sat in the cask room, preparing corks for the full wine bottles. She felt a bit tipsy from the alcoholic fumes floating through the warm air. The repetitive work and the fragrance of the fermenting wine did not prepare her for what came next. It was mid-afternoon when suddenly she felt something wet pouring onto her feet. She knew it wasn't grape juice! The baby was on its way!

She waddled over to the doorway and shouted for Signora Bianca. The chubby Italian lady came running. "Il bambino! Il bambino!" she shouted with joy.

Before the night was over on September 19, 1937, a little boy came into the world. It was Erev Sukkot, the Jewish harvest festival. There would be no welcoming of this little boy into the Covenant since there was no *mohel* anywhere near the Fermi farm. Since there was no *bris*, the baby boy didn't get a Hebrew name either. But because his parents were so fond of the German Jewish poet Heinrich Heine, they gave him the name Enrico, which is Italian for Heinrich.

After a week of rest, Herta returned to work in the bottling area. Enrico lay in a manger in an empty horse stall within earshot. Signora Bianca said he was just like Jesus: they were two beautiful little Jewish boys, asleep in the hay.

Herta wrote her parents immediately with the good news. There was no letter in response. She wrote again to give them an update on Enrico's growth and progress. Again, no reply. Nearly a year went by. Finally, a letter came. It had taken weeks to arrive instead of the usual five or six days.

September 19, 1938
Tauhaubischelstein

Dearest Herta, Abie, and Enrico,

There is no excuse for my failure to write you in over a year. But I will take the chance now since it is little Enrico's birthday. Yes, your letter about his birth reached us, but ever since then, the Nazis are reading our mail. Not every letter, but most of it. I didn't want them to know where you and Abie are, in case they start looking for him in Italy.

Papa and I are so happy for you to have such a healthy boy. I know you are a good mother and it gives me a great peace of mind to know that. That is the only thing that gives me peace.

It is only a matter of time before the Nazis take over the factory and the business completely. By the end of the year, we certainly will be thrown out of it, and then? Who knows what will happen to us. We have no visa to go anywhere. The Nazis will not let us leave Germany anyway. We will end up going somewhere they will send us.

I want you all to know that we love you and will always love you. Wherever we go, if we survive until Hitler is gone from Germany, we will try to find you when we return to our home. May God bless and keep you all.

With everlasting love from your parents
Max and Selma Sauer

Herta took the letter and immediately showed it to Abie. He read it and shrugged his shoulders.

"What can we do?" he said, sadly.

"What can WE do?" she responded, angrily. "It's what YOU can do! You can smuggle them into Italy!"

CHAPTER THIRTEEN

PREPARING FOR A DARING RESCUE

The harvest was complete at the Fermi vineyard. The wine was aging in casks, waiting to be poured into bottles. It was a good time for the Cohens to have a talk with the Fermis.

Herta invited Signor Giuseppe and Signora Bianca to breakfast, something she'd never done before. The night before, she prepared dough to make challah rolls for breakfast – a real treat for everyone. After everyone had eaten, she put Enrico down for a nap and invited the older couple onto the patio.

She showed them the letter from her parents. Signor Giuseppe didn't speak German very well, but he was a good reader. He explained the message to his wife. Bianca started crying. Over the years, she and Selma had become good friends.

"What can we do?" Giuseppe asked.

Herta hardly had slept the night before. Her mind was whirring. How could they sneak her parents out of Germany without alerting the Nazis? Who should be involved? What steps were realistic? What was safe? What was dangerous? What was impossible?

She described her plan point by point. No one asked questions. She had thought of every detail.

"Will you help us, Signor Giuseppe?" she asked. "There's no other way without your help and cooperation."

Signor Giuseppe looked at his wife. She nodded.

"Your family has been more than just paying guests to us," he said to Herta. "You are close friends. You and Abie have helped us with our crop when our neighbors tried to take advantage of us. Let's do it!"

The first thing they needed to do was to get something for Abie that looked like a legitimate Italian identification card.

"We will ask Signor Michele if he has any business contacts in the printing business," Herta stated calmly. "Can we drive into Milan today? I think that the Sciamas would love to see Enrico, too!"

Signor Giuseppe, Abie, Herta and little Enrico piled into the Fermi farm truck for the two-hour drive to Milan so that they would be there right after lunch. Signor Michele always ate lunch at home.

They pulled up to the Sciama house shortly after one. Signora Rebeca opened the door and squealed with delight to see Enrico standing, holding his father's hand. She swept up the toddler and invited everyone into the living room.

Signor Michele heard the commotion and entered into the room, saying, "Send that little one over to me!"

There was much hugging and shaking of hands.

In a minute, when everyone was seated, Herta pulled out the letter and showed it to Signor Michele. He read it, handed it to his wife, and sat in stunned silence. He looked up and turned to Herta, "What can we do to help?"

Herta sighed with relief. "Grazie! We are going to smuggle them out. We have never told you, but Abie is in Italy with illegal papers from Holland. They are expired, anyway. We need to get him documents that look like he is an Italian citizen."

Signor Michele put his hand over his eyes, as if he was trying to remember something from long ago. After a moment, he looked up. "I will send you with a letter to Camillo Olivetti in Ivrea, near Turin."

"Olivetti?" Abie asked, "The people who make typewriters?"

"Yes, and they also do printing." Signor Michele continued, "They are Jews. I hear that they have been making counterfeit documents for Jews fleeing Hitler."

"How much does he charge?" Abie had no idea of the value of Herta's gold and jewels. He'd never looked inside the bag.

"I have no idea," Signor Michele replied. "We have done a little business with them over the years. I will give you a letter of introduction. Perhaps he will not charge you too much."

Everyone heaved a sigh of relief. They could cross off the first item on Herta's list.

Signor Michele excused himself to go to his study and write the letter. The rest went into the garden to play with Enrico. Signor Michele returned in a few minutes with two envelopes.

"This one is the introduction," he said, handing Abie the first envelope. "And this one has some money in it. It will be a *mitzvah* for me to pay whatever it may cost."

Herta was not the kind to show emotion in public, but she threw her arms around Signor Michele's neck and hugged him as hard as she could.

"We will never be able to thank you enough. Someday we will find a way to repay you!"

Signor Michele waved her away.

"No need, no need! You have become like a daughter to us, Herta. Your father has been a good person to do business with all these years and I respect him greatly. Buona fortuna!" he said, and opened the door for them to leave.

Back in the truck, Herta looked at Signor Giuseppe and asked, "What's the best way to get to Ivrea?"

The next morning, Abie and Signor Giuseppe climbed back into the truck and drove west. The Fermis had a customer there and knew the town well. No one would think it unusual to see his truck pull into the Olivetti factory lot. He dropped Abie off at the office door.

"I'm going to stop over to see my customer," he said, "I've brought him a bottle of my new wine to try. I'll pick you up in three hours. Buona fortuna!"

Abie pushed open the office door. A receptionist sat at a big desk.

"I am here to see Signor Camillo Olivetti," he said, twisting his cap in his hands, trying to hide his nervousness. "I have a letter of introduction from Signor Michele Sciama in Milan."

The receptionist nodded. "Just a minute. I know he is on the telephone right now. Perhaps he can give you a minute when he is done." She went inside an office with "Camillo Olivetti, Presidente" on the door's frosted glass window.

In a minute, she returned, "He will see you in a few minutes." She gestured for Abie to take a seat nearby. They were some of the longest minutes Abie ever waited in his life.

The door opened. A very handsome man with silver hair in an elegant suit stepped out.

"Benvenuto! Come in. Any friend of Michele Sciama is my friend!" he proclaimed with Italian gusto.

In addition to the two envelopes from Signor Michele, Abie had the letter from the Sauers in Germany. First, he handed over the one from Milan. Signor Olivetti, read it and his face grew serious. When he was done, Abie was quick to hand him the other letter. When Signor Olivetti read the awful story, his face turned sad.

"You need my help to rescue these people, correct?" he asked Abie, who was trembling with fear that he would be turned away.

"Yes, sir," Abie replied, humbly. "I need papers to get into Germany and out again."

What Signor Olivetti said next shocked the younger man. "How fast do you need them?"

"As soon as possible, sir. You can see that the situation of my wife's parents is dangerous."

"And what do you want these papers to say?"

"Sir, I want them to say that I am the son of Signor Giuseppe Fermi. He is helping us with our plot. He has been a friend to my wife's family for years. He is willing to help with their rescue, at risk of his own life. We are living with him and his wife right now. Signor Giuseppe brought me here today."

"Come with me," Signor Olivetti commanded. "Hold all of my calls for the next two hours," he told the receptionist.

The two men went onto the factory floor, filled with printing presses of all sizes. In less than two hours, Abie held an Italian identification card bearing the name "Carlo Fermi" with his photograph and several official-looking stamps.

"You have never met me," Signor Olivetti stated, looking Abie directly in the eyes.

"I swear it," Abie replied. "With my life, I swear it."

"Bene," Signor Olivetti said, and shook Abie's hand. "And now for my payment!"

Abie breathed in hard and held his breath, waiting for the next statement.

"And my payment will be a case of Signor Fermi's best wine!"

They both laughed with relief. "That is not a problem, Signor!"

The payment was made when the Fermi truck drove up shortly afterward.

CHAPTER FOURTEEN

A PERILOUS MISSION

Abie was terrified of crossing into Germany. Signor Giuseppe suggested that they drive through Switzerland instead of through France to test the quality of the forged document. He had a customer in Winterthur, near the border. He could deliver some wine there en route to Tauhaubischelstein.

The two men loaded the truck first with two empty casks that had never been filled with wine. They went in the back of the truck. Then, they filled it nearly to the top with crate upon crate of bottled wine.

As they loaded the last crates into the truck, Signor Giuseppe commented to Abie with a laugh, "These last bottles I always save to use to thank border guards for their service."

Abie knew that Signor Giuseppe really meant that the wine was used to bribe them.

Abie could see that his wife was scared. He could see that she tried to put on a happy, brave face as she and Signora Bianca bid him and Signor Giuseppe "buona fortuna" as they climbed into the truck. Herta held up little Enrico for his father's last kiss.

If Herta was scared, Abie was petrified. Would he be leaving her and Enrico to a life as a widow and orphan?

The truck pulled out and headed north into the Alps. This was a dangerous time. Winter was upon them and roads might be closed due to heavy snowfall. Would an avalanche stop their progress?

Signor Giuseppe sang Italian folk songs to lift their spirits. Yes, there was snow, but the sun was bright upon it. Its sparkling brilliance on the white mountainsides sometimes made it hard to see the road. They journeyed on.

Here was the Swiss border. Here was a border guard.

Giuseppe whispered to Abie, "Speak as little as possible. Your accent will give you away."

The guard asked for their identification, and looked at the truck.

"Ahhh! Wine from Italy! Isn't our Swiss wine good enough?"

Abie sat quietly as Signor Giuseppe jumped down from behind the wheel and walked to the back of the truck. Abie watched what happened in the rear-view mirror.

"Here," said Signor Giussepe, handing the guard a bottle. "It is already nicely chilled here in the snowy mountains. You can decide for yourself which wine is best!"

And so, the two "Italians" passed through the gate into Switzerland.

It was dark by the time they reached Winterthur. It looked a lot like Germany to Abie's eyes.

The two men stopped the truck near a building close to the center of town.

"I always stay here when I come to Winterthur," Signor Giuseppe commented.

He knocked on the door and in a minute it opened. Abie heard happy conversation in a mix of Italian and German. Signor Giuseppe motioned to Abie to come in. They were led up a stairway to a small room with two beds. Abie felt the same as when he first arrived in Milan and shared Carlo Bottazzi's room there. He was emotionally exhausted. Clearly, Signor Giuseppe felt the same. They said little, washed up, and collapsed onto the beds.

There was a good breakfast waiting for them in the morning, but Abie hardly ate a bite. His stomach was in knots. He was thinking about the next hurdle: crossing into Germany.

The southern border town, Kreuzlingen, was far from Aurich in the north. It had been more than three years since the terrible accident there. Pictures from the newspaper would have been forgotten. No one would recognize him. He hoped.

"Guten tag!" said the German border guard to the two men. He wore a Nazi pin on the lapel of his winter jacket. "May I see your papers, bitte?"

Signor Giuseppe handed over both sets of paper.

"Father and son?" the guard asked, raising an eyebrow.

"Si, si!" Signor Giuseppe said. "I'm bringing my strong, young son to help me lift the heavy crates full of wine bottles!"

"May I see your cargo?"

"Ovviamente!" he replied, politely. He turned to Abie. "You stay here and keep the engine running. It's cold and I don't want to have trouble starting it up again."

Abie knew this was a hint that they might have to make a quick getaway.

Signor Giuseppe opened the cargo door. The guard shined a flashlight around it.

"What's that in the back?" he asked.

"Ah, those are vats that I sell to big hotels. I bring a full vat and take home the empty one from my last visit."

The answer seemed to satisfy the guard. He looked again at the papers. He looked at Abie, who gave a little, friendly wave. "Well, all seems to be in order. Drive carefully. There is ice on many of the roads."

Abie leaned over to open the door for Signor Giuseppe to climb back into the truck's cab. They drove off slowly. Abie and Signor Giussepe looked at each other. They both sighed and then smiled. Herta's plan and Signor Olivetti's papers were working.

On they drove to Stuttgart, just a father and son who were wine merchants doing their regular rounds to deliver to their customers. They waited at a customer's restaurant in a small town until it grew dark. An illuminated road sign pointed them to Tauhaubischelstein and the truck was turned in that direction.

Abie had a map that Herta had drawn for them. There it was: the Sauer home, at a dead end of a short street. The street was deserted and had only two streetlights at the half-way point. Signor Giuseppe maneuvered the truck so that the loading gate faced the door of the Sauer home. Abie sat as a lookout while Signor Giuseppe got out, walked to the back of the truck, and opened the loading gate.

He stuck his head into the truck's cab and told Abie, "I'll take it from here. The Sauers know me, but they certainly will not recognize you as Herta's husband and may be hesitant to open the door for you."

Abie nodded in agreement. How awful it might be if his in-laws refused entry to him, a stranger in the dark of the night.

Signor Giuseppe turned and knocked on the door. It was late. The Sauers would not be expecting visitors – except, perhaps, some Nazis making trouble. He turned to look at Abie and shrugged his shoulders. Turning back, he knocked again and shouted, "It's me, Giuseppe! I've got the wine you ordered!"

In a moment, the door opened a crack. Max looked out and saw his friend from the light in the hallway. The door opened wide. Giuseppe entered and Max tried to closed the door, but Giuseppe put his foot in the entry, leaned out and waved to Abie to come in. Abie could hear their words.

"What are you doing here?" Max asked, shaking his friend's hand vigorously. "Selma, come to the door! Giuseppe Fermi is here!"

Selma came to the doorway and gave Giuseppe a hug. "What are you doing here? Is it about Herta? Is it about Enrico?"

Signor Giuseppe chuckled and opened the door to let Abie enter. "Here is your son-in-law Abie to deliver their greetings in person."

The Sauers looked at each other, confused. They looked at Abie. Without a word, the strangers embraced as family.

Giuseppe continued, "Abie and I are here to smuggle you into Italy."

Max and Selma Sauer were speechless. Giuseppe filled in the silence.

"Now, rush. Go and get a few things – just a change of clothes – that you can put into one small bag each. Wear your warmest coats. Go quickly. You are sure to have some Nazi sympathizers as neighbors and if they wake up and see this truck, they will suspect something. Go!"

The Sauers quickly climbed the stairs. Abie could hear drawers being opened and closed. Then, there was a little discussion in loud voices. Within five minutes, the Sauers stood in the hallway, each with a small satchel.

Signor Giuseppe took Selma's bag.

"What's so heavy in here? I told you to bring just a change of clothes."

Max and Selma looked at each other. Then Max gestured for Selma to speak.

"It is my Sabbath candlesticks," she admitted, sticking out her chin defiantly. "They have been in my mother's family for over 300 years and I will not leave them behind!"

Max started to open his mouth to protest, but Selma continued, "Yes, they are heavy. I can use them to hit a Nazi over the head if he doesn't see me coming from behind!"

Giuseppi laughed, "Well, as long as they fit in that bag, you can take them. Let's go!"

Abie took Max's bag and put his arm around his father-in-law's shoulders as they walked to the back of the truck. He lifted his mother-in-law onto its wooden floor. Max pulled himself up and stood next to his wife.

Signor Giuseppi shined a flashlight onto two very large casks.

"These are empty. You are the fine wine that will fill them. There is a hole in each of them where the spigot should go. That is for your air."

He climbed on an empty crate and pulled the top off of the casks. Abie helped them each into their separate hiding place, dropped in their bags, and replaced the tops.

"Everyone okay?" Abie asked. "Knock once for yes, twice for no."

One knock came from inside each cask.

Abie and Signor Giuseppi moved the crates with empty bottles that some customers had returned. The bottles in the crates clinked against each other, masking any noise that might come from within the vats. There was no noise coming from them anyway.

Abie remembered his grief at leaving Aurich in haste. Now he imagined how the Sauers were left with their thoughts of the house and the town they were leaving, unable to take a last look. He was surrounded by fear of being discovered at the border, if not sooner. Abie's heart was full of thanks to this man who was risking his life to save the lives of people with whom he shared no blood or national loyalty. Abie's gratitude was even greater since his fate would likely be worse than what the Sauers might face if the truck's secret contents were discovered.

The truck moved slowly through the streets of Tauhaubischelstein. The dim street lights stood like guards to protect this couple who had spent their entire lives within its borders.

Abie and Signor Giuseppe were checking off more points on Herta's plan. Did she really plan for everything? What if something went wrong?

Once out of town, Signor Giuseppe turned the wheel over to Abie. It would be good to sleep a bit before they reached the border. They'd cross into Switzerland at the same place and hope that the same guard was on duty.

A few miles before the border, they traded places again. When they pulled to the side of the road, Abie opened the cargo gate and spoke to the crates, bottles and casks inside, "One if all's well. Two if there's a problem."

One thump came from each cask.

The lights at the border crossing seemed exceptionally bright. There were two guards, both with rifles. The fugitives stopped at the gate, as far from the little building as possible. It was very cold. They could see a guard approaching.

"Papers, bitte," the guard asked, sternly. He had a Nazi pin on his coat lapel, like the other guard. He looked at the papers. Giuseppe showed receipts for the wine he'd delivered. All very legitimate. The guard looked at the identification papers. Twice.

"Just a minute," he said, casting an eye on Abie's face, which he tried to hide with his cap. "I need to check something inside."

This was not good, Abie thought. Signor Giuseppe reached over and opened the glove compartment by Abie's knees. There was a pistol inside. Signor Giuseppe grabbed it, closed the compartment, and put the gun under his thigh. Abie was trembling. He wanted to rush out and kick the guards like he had kicked the policeman in Aurich. Instead, he sat still.

Just before the guard entered the building, the other guard came out of it. There was some discussion. The two guards turned around and walked toward the truck.

As they approached, the men in the car heard a familiar voice, "Guten abend, meine freunde!"

It was the guard who'd let them pass into Germany.

"My friend shows me your papers and you did good business in Germany!" he said, laughing. "Did you sell everything or did you save a couple bottles for me and my friend?"

"Of course we did!" Signor Giuseppe replied, also laughing through his fear. "Carlo, reach behind the seat and pull out those bottles we've saved!"

Abie did as he was told. Four bottles of white wine with the Fermi Farm label on them. He handed them to Signor Giuseppe who gave them to the guard.

"We still need to take a look in the truck," the friendly guard said.

Abie watched as Signor Giuseppe took off his cap to hide the pistol as he opened the door to step out. They walked to the back and opened the gate. The guard shined his flashlight. Abie could hear them talking.

"Empty bottles, yawohl," the friendly guard commented. "And the casks. They don't look like they've been used."

"They've been used," Signor Giuseppe replied. "They had white wine in them and they do not stain as if they had been storing red."

The guards seemed satisfied with that explanation.

"You can get back in the truck," the guard announced. "We'll open the gate. Don't forget me on your next time through this border point!"

The truck rolled on. The Swiss border guards accepted more bottles of wine. Another check-off for Herta's list.

As dawn broke, the truck stopped just before a small town beyond Winterthur. Abie helped Signor Giuseppe move the crates around. He climbed up and pulled the tops off the casks. He and Signor Giuseppe helped Max and Selma to climb out.

There was much hugging and laughing! They'd escaped! They'd pulled it off! There was only one more border to cross. The Sauers had brought their identification papers. They hoped that the Italian border guards would let them pass, even though the papers were stamped "Jude." Of course, there were still quite a few bottles of wine stashed behind Abie's seat in the truck to deal with that problem!

It was a bit cramped in the truck's cab with the four travellers all sitting together, watching the road without fear of being seen. They didn't care. They were alive and on their way to see people they all loved. The travellers stopped at an inn by the side of the road to have a good meal and freshen up. They would not stay the night. The Sauer parents would sit comfortably up front in the truck as Abie and Signor Giuseppe took turns driving and the other sat with the cargo.

At the Swiss border, no problems and a bottle of wine just to make sure.

The Italian border station was only a kilometer away. The guard waved them through without asking for identification. Why should he? The truck had Italian license plates. The letters painted on the truck that said "Fermi Farm" declared to all that the owner was Italian. Everyone waved at the guards and shouted "Grazie!"

They had made it! Safety and family lay ahead. Or so they thought.

CHAPTER FIFTEEN

SEEKING A SAFE HAVEN

When the truck pulled up the path to the little villa on the Fermi farm, Herta stood at the doorway with a worried look on her face, holding Enrico's hand. Her expression turned to joy when she saw who stepped out of it: Mama, Papa, and Signor Giuseppe. She ran toward them with Enrico toddling after her. They hugged until they seemed one person.

Then Herta looked up. Where was Abie? Had he been caught by the Nazis for his crime in Aurich so long ago? No. The gate on the back of the truck was stuck and it took Signor Giuseppe and Max together to push it high enough for Abie to crawl out. There was more joy!

The travellers were all hungry and dirty. Signora Bianca showed Max and Selma to the villa next door to shower and change clothes. Everyone was invited to the Fermi house for a celebration afterward.

It was New Year's Eve day. The travellers told of their dangerous trip. They laughed at how easily the German guards could be bribed with just a couple bottles of wine. They toasted Herta for her marvelous plan. They toasted Signor Giuseppe for his cunning trickery with the Germans. They toasted Abie for his courage in returning to Germany, at the risk of being discovered as a wanted criminal. They toasted Enrico – just because. Everyone toasted what they hoped would be safety, health, and prosperity in 1939.

It wasn't. Mussolini had followed Hitler's example and in 1938 passed laws that discriminated against Jews. The Cohens already felt the effects of the laws when they were in Milan, but out in the country on the Fermi farm, everything seemed peaceful. But they knew they couldn't stay there forever. Their future elsewhere in Italy seemed as bleak as in Milan. America was not a possibility. Where could they go?

Signor Giuseppe always went into Milan during the first week of each month to go to the bank and get supplies. Abie and Max started going with him. Abie remembered that there were consulates from all over the world in the streets near the University.

In January, they went to consulates for countries in Europe and Scandinavia. None of them would even accept an application.

The family discussed the possibility of South Africa. They knew that country had a sizeable Jewish population. But the idea of Africa frightened Selma.

In February, they went to the consulates for Mexico and Cuba. These consulates would not consider them because Abie did not have legal documents with his own name on them.

In March, they tried Argentina, another country with a large Jewish population. But Argentina was allied with Germany and would not accept refugees like the Sauers from there. They would take the Cohens because Enrico was an Italian citizen. But the family wanted to stay together.

The clerk in the consulate of Mexico in April told them that they would be able to make an application, but the fee would be $5,000 in American money – for each of them! Max and Abie knew that the clerk was really asking for a bribe. Max knew that $25,000 was far beyond what Herta's jewelry and coins were worth. They walked away, without even trying to bargain.

Near the end of the street was a flag that the men didn't recognize. It had yellow, blue and red horizontal stripes with some sort of embroidered medallion in the center. There was a plaque on the door that read "Consulate of the Republic of Ecuador." The men looked at each other. "Why not give it a try?" Abie suggested to his father-in-law.

"I've never heard of the place, but what choice do we have?" Max replied.

The two men entered the lobby and saw an office with a sign for the Consulate of Ecuador on it. They entered and saw a well-dressed gentleman seated behind a desk in a small reception area. There was the flag, two framed maps – one of Ecuador and one of South America, another small desk and chair, and some file cabinets and a couple more chairs.

The man stood up and extended his hand. "Welcome to the Consulate of Ecuador. I am Emilio Zorer. Please sit down." He spoke in Italian.

Abie and Max took seats. They looked at the maps. Now they knew where Ecuador is in the world.

"We would like to talk to the Consul," Abie said.

Señor Zorer chuckled. "I *am* the Consul," he said proudly. "We have a very small staff here. How can I help you? Do you wish to take a tour of Ecuador?"

"Sort of. We want to be permanent tourists in your country. We want to live in Ecuador!"

Señor Zorer sat silently and looked at them. The men were nervous. Was Ecuador friendly to the Nazis and Fascists? They had no idea.

"Are you Jews?"

Max answered with no hesitation, "Yes, we are Jews. We are fleeing from Hitler."

"Good!" Señor Zorer replied. That was a surprise to Abie and Max. "It is a part of our Ecuadorian Constitution to be welcoming to refugees."

Abie and Max looked at each other in amazement. Why hadn't they heard about this place before?

"Is there anything special that we must do to apply for visas?" Max asked. He remembered the bribe that the Mexican clerk wanted them to pay.

"Well, the application fee is $250 American per person."

Abie and Max nodded their heads. They could afford that.

Señor Zorer continued, "We have been accepting refugees since Hitler first came to power. All of the early refugees came with lots of money and have started some successful businesses."

"We don't have much money," Abie said, sadly.

"That's fine," Señor Zorer said, calmly. "What we are looking for now is people who know about farming."

Abie almost fainted, he was so relieved. He knew he wouldn't have to lie when he said, "I have been working at a vineyard in the Brescia province for the past year. I know everything about that business! I can even provide you with references from my employer, Giuseppe Fermi."

"That should help," the Consul said, nodding his head. "I don't know if this is the kind of farming we're looking for, but it should be good enough. Once your visas are approved, you will be assigned to an hacienda somewhere in Ecuador. Most of them are near major cities."

"I have one more important question," Abie started. "I do not have any legal documents, but my wife and her parents," he said, pointing to Max, "have everything you'll want. My son Enrico has an Italian birth certificate."

"Not a problem," Señor Zorer shook his head. "Many refugees do not have papers. Perhaps someone here in Milan will swear an oath that you are who you say you are."

"Ah!" Max exclaimed. "Michele Sciama can do that!"

Señor Zorer reached into a file cabinet and handed them five copies of several different forms. "Do you have a schedule for travel?" he asked.

Max and Abie looked at each other again. They really hadn't thought of this.

"As soon as possible, Signor," Abie replied, surprising even himself. "If you know how we can arrange transportation, it would help us set a timetable."

"There are no cruise ships to Ecuador from Italy," the Consul explained. "All travellers and refugees can book rooms on freighters that go from Genoa to Guayaquil, but there are very few available on each ship. They're very comfortable," he assured them. "It's how I travel myself!" He pulled out another document that told which ships sailed between the two countries.

With their hands full of documents, the two Jewish refugees thanked the kind gentleman from Ecuador and headed out onto the street. They looked at all of the flags lining it. None of those other countries wanted them. Ecuador did.

CHAPTER SIXTEEN

PREPARATIONS AND THE BOY GETS HIS SECOND NAME

The next few days were spent by the family poring over the documents that Abie and Max brought back to the Fermi farm. Photos needed to be taken. Forms had to be filled out, honestly. At least, they didn't have to figure out what to take with them and what to leave in Italy. They owned very little more than the clothes on their backs, the jewelry in the safe-deposit box, and each other.

It was the beginning of May. They decided to make the trip in June. Max had bought an almanac. It reported that hurricane season in the Caribbean Sea starts in late May and went through September, so the threat to their boat being hit by a hurricane were not so great in June as later in the summer. That gave them nearly two months to prepare if they caught a boat late in the month.

They already had learned that Herta was a wonderful planner. They would not be together that day if she had not planned every step of the process to smuggle her parents out of Germany. Herta now had two jobs: To cash in more of her jewelry to pay expenses, and to make the plan. She would leave the others to carry out the plan and she could dedicate herself to Enrico's care. As a toddler, he was a handful now!

Selma was to make sure that all of their clothing was mended and clean. She took care of the villas until they left.

Abie would continue working with the Fermis. It was spring, 1939 and the grape vines were blooming.

Max's job was to make sure that every detail needed for them to leave Italy safely and legally was in order. He was a businessman and knew how to deal with government agents and other businessmen.

The next Wednesday in May, Herta drove into Milan with Signor Giuseppe. She got off at the Banca Monte dei Paschi and walked in confidently. She always went to the same teller.

"Buongiorno!" she greeted the teller.

Without another word, the teller reached into her drawer, took out a key and gestured for Herta to follow her into the vault with safe deposit boxes. Herta took out her precious bag with its even more precious contents and peeked in. Yes, it seemed to be all there. She closed the box, turned and walked back to the teller's window.

"Grazie," Herta began. "I am here to end my rental of the box."

"At your service," the teller replied. "I will not charge you rent for the rest of this month. Is there anything else I can help with?

Herta nodded, "And I want to close my account here. Can you please give me most of it in American dollars?"

"There will be a small charge for the dollars."

Herta nodded again. The teller stepped away and Herta waited for a few minutes. When the teller returned, she explained the value of the dollars as they compared to Italian liras. Then, she leaned over the counter and whispered quietly to Herta, "Can you tell me why you need over $2,000 dollars?"

Herta leaned in toward the teller. "We are leaving Italy for good. We are going to Ecuador."

"I know that you are a Jew since your last name is Cohen." The teller reached into her collar and pulled out a small Jewish star on a gold chain. "I am, too. My family wants to leave Italy as well, but we have heard that almost no one will take refugees who are not wealthy. Shall we try the Ecuadorian consulate?"

Herta nodded, and reached out her hand to shake the teller's hand. "Buona fortuna! And shalom!"

She walked to Signor Finzi's jewelry store to sell another small piece. She would use the liras for the family to live on until leaving Italy. She thanked Signor Finzi for always giving her a good price and told him why she sold the gold and pearl pin.

"Ecuador?" he asked. "In South America? They're still taking Jews?"

"Si, Signor, if you are willing to work in agriculture."

Signor Finzi thought for a moment. "I cannot say that I have done anything more than plant a flower in a pot. I will have to look elsewhere. Buona fortuna!"

She walked back to the Banca Monte dei Paschi, sat in a sidewalk café next door and waited for Signor Giuseppe to return.

Everyone did their part. Even Enrico did his part by not crying much or begging for attention.

At the beginning of June, the entire family rode into Milan on the Fermi Farm truck and got off at the Ecuadorian consulate. Michele Sciama was waiting for them on the sidewalk. They walked in together.

Señor Zorer was at his desk, and a woman now was sitting at the other desk.

"Buenos dias!" he exclaimed in Spanish. "Is this the whole family now?"

Everyone introduced themselves, except for Enrico who couldn't talk anything other than babbling.

"And do you have all the necessary documents and photos filled out?"

Max handed over the paperwork and checked them for blank lines and signatures.

"And Signor Sciama is here to swear that the man claiming to be Abraham Cohen is indeed that person?"

"Si, Señor Zorer," Signor Michele replied. "I have brought a Jewish bible to swear upon!"

Señor Zorer snorted and then chuckled. "We don't really need a bible. Your oath will be good enough."

Señor Zorer asked Signor Michele to affirm the truth of all the questions about Abie. The answer to each of them was a loud "Si!"

"You are in luck," Señor Zorer replied, "our secretary is here today and she can type up and seal your passports while you wait."

He handed the paperwork over to the secretary.

"And now for your travel," he said, pulling out more paper from the drawers in his small desk.

The family had decided to travel with the first boat with space available from Genoa. Was there anything still open in June?

Señor Zorer looked through the papers. The ship *Pacha Mama* would leave from Genoa on June 18. There were two staterooms available. The deposit would be $50 per room. He would give them receipts and vouchers to pay the remainder when they reached the dock. Herta reached into her purse and gave him $100 in liras.

"Is that okay?" Herta asked. She had not planned for this expense in dollars. One mistake. She was afraid she may have made others in the plan. She crossed her fingers.

"Fine," Señor Zorer replied and held out his hand. He wrote up a receipt and two vouchers for tickets that had to be paid in dollars.

The secretary was done with her task. She handed the passports over to Señor Zorer. He handed them to each of their new owners, even to Enrico who immediately put it in his mouth!

Herta snatched it away, and looked inside the booklet. She was shocked.

"What is this?" she exclaimed. "It says his name is Enrique!"

Señor Zorer replied with a big smile, "You can call him what you want. But if he is going to be raised in Ecuador, he needs an Ecuadorian name. Enrique is Spanish for Enrico. It's been sealed, so in his new country he will officially be Enrique. And since you are unhappy, I will not charge you for his passport."

Herta sighed. This was a small bonus in exchange for agreeing to the Spanish name. She reached into her purse and gave Señor Zorer $1,000. Everyone shook hands.

"Oh, I almost forgot," Señor Zorer said, "You need to know where you will be living in Ecuador. You will be living in the city of Riobamba and Señor Abraham will be assigned to work at an hacienda in the area."

The family looked at each other and shrugged their shoulders. They'd never heard of Riobamba. But they'd never heard of any city in Ecuador either. As long as they were far from Hitler and Mussolini, they were happy.

"Adios y buena suerte!" he called to them as they closed the office door.

CHAPTER SEVENTEEN

JOURNEY TO A NEW HOMELAND

The days flew by. They hardly noticed the blossoming summer at the Fermi farm. Now that their arrangements were set, the whole family did their all to help the Fermis with every part of the vineyard. They wanted to show their tremendous appreciation for all that this unselfish couple had done to save them from Hitler's hate.

Early on the morning of June 18, 1939, everyone – even Signora Bianca – piled into the truck to go to the Milan train station. They were surprised to find Carlo Bottazzi waiting for them. There were only four suitcases among the five family members. The train to Genoa was set for 10:00 a.m. and the Pacha Mama was scheduled to sail at 5:00 p.m. There was plenty of time, unless something went wrong with Herta's plan.

There were many tears and even more embraces as the two groups – Italians and Jews — stood on the platform waiting for the conductor to shout "Tutti abordo!" It came too soon, even though the the train was on time when the clock struck ten.

"Addio! Addio! We will write!" everyone promised. And everyone knew those promises would be broken quickly.

Enrique loved watching the landscape go by on the train. It made two stops before it wheezed into the terminal in Genoa. A line of taxis was waiting outside. Abie grabbed one and helped the driver load the suitcases.

"To the marina!" he instructed the driver, and consulted his ticket voucher for the hundredth time. "Wharf 18!"

The driver sped through traffic and screeched his brakes to a halt at Wharf 18. The family carried their bags down the wharf until they came to Dock 36. There was an ugly ship with peeling paint on it. On the bow were the words "Pacha Mama" and Salinas, Ecuador. This was it.

A sunburned man in a blue uniform looked over the railing and shouted to them in Italian, "Are you the Cohen-Sauer family?"

They all shouted back a loud "Si!"

The man disappeared and then they saw him start down the gangway. They walked over to meet him.

"Benvenuti! Bienvenidos!" he said, extending a friendly hand. "I am Fausto Venegas, Captain of the *Pacha Mama*. Come with me, please."

Captain Venegas grabbed Selma's bag and seemed surprised at how heavy it was. Her Shabbos candlesticks were inside, of course. They all followed him up the gangway into his office in the wheel house.

"May I see your vouchers and passports?" he asked politely.

Abie handed them over. "Is everything in order?"

Captain Venegas leafed throught the documents. "One hundred percent. All that is left is for you to pay the balance for your voyage in dollars." He pointed to an amount on the receipt.

Herta reached into her purse, which was also heavy. She kept her jewelry bag with her at all times. She counted out a handful of bills, "This is the correct amount, isn't it?"

Captain Venegas counted them. "Yes! I see you have more dollars. You can change them into Ecuadorian currency at the port in Salinas." He turned to the rest. "Would you like to see your rooms? The other family traveling with us has arrived already. We shall all meet for dinner at 7:00 p.m. in the Captain's dining room."

The family dutifully followed Captain Venegas down a flight of stairs and into a short hallway with doors on both sides. He stopped and opened one for them to look inside. It was small with two beds, one with a bunk bed over it and a porthole. Bath towels hung on a bar on the cabin door. There was a basket of fruit on the single bed, too. What a nice welcome!

"This should work well for you with little," he paused to think for a moment, "little Enrique."

The Cohens picked up their bags and stepped inside. The Sauers would be next door. There was a communal bathroom at the end of the hall.

There was no room to unpack their bags, so they just shoved them under the beds. This certainly wasn't a luxurious ocean liner, but it was cheap and clean and would take them where they wanted to go. Safely, they hoped.

After they took turns washing up, the family went upstairs and sat on deckchairs, enjoying the fruit and the clear salt air. Everyone fell asleep. Saying goodbye to the Fermis had exhausted them emotionally.

At 5:00 p.m., on the dot, a steam whistle blew loudly, waking them up. Sailors appeared from below decks to haul in the ropes that tied the *Pacha Mama* to the dock. The ship pulled out into the Mediterranean Sea, taking the refugees with them. Would they ever return to Europe? If so, when? But no one shed a tear. The Europe of Hitler and Mussolini was not the Europe they loved, at least not right then.

Seven o'clock came and a friendly sailor showed them to the Captain's dining room. Although the hull and decks of the *Pacha Mama* were industrial, this room was elegant. The walls were covered with rich-looking wood, delicate curtains covered the portholes, and the table was set with fine china and silver. Captain Venegas was waiting for them and invited them to take seats.

In walked the other passengers. They were dressed elegantly, as if for a fancy banquet. There were parents and two boys in their early teens. They spoke a strange language.

"Jacob Mugasey," the gentleman introduced himself, extending his hand to Max. He went on to point to the others in his family, "Szofia, Tamas, Laszlo."

They were from Hungary, en route to the *Pacha Mama*'s first port-of-call, Havana, Cuba. They didn't speak Italian and only a little German, but they spoke English quite well. The Cohens and Sauers spoke German and Italian, but no English. None of them spoke Spanish, but that was the language that Captain Venegas spoke best. There was not a lot of conversation over the dinner table. But the food was good, so no one complained.

It would take four days to reach Havana. Lack of a common language did not stop the adults from playing card games and dominos to entertain each other. The Captain's dining room held a shelf for books in several languages, including an Italian-Spanish dictionary. The Cohens and Sauers spent many hours with that.

The person who enjoyed the voyage most was Enrique. The sailors aboard the *Pacha Mama* adopted him as their mascot. Enrique was just starting to pronounce syllables that he'd heard in Italian and German. It was quite a surprise then, when at dinner just before they reached Havana that the little boy looked up from his beans and said, "Enrique!" Everyone clapped and showed him how happy they were.

Then he said another word. Only Captain Venegas understood it and he grew very angry. He jumped up from the table and ran to call his first mate.

"Who taught this boy to say that horrible word in Spanish?" he demanded, and then he started laughing.

The first mate's face turned red. He made a remark to the Captain, saluted him, and left the room.

"Let us just hope that he forgets that word before we reach Salinas," Captain Venegas said.

There was no hurricane. There was one day of light rain on the endless Atlantic. It was hard to keep a toddler occupied in the tiny stateroom, but a small taste of wine goes a long way to keep a little boy sleeping.

The Mugasey family left the ship in Havana. The crew carried off numerous trunks, crates, and suitcases for them. Clearly, the Mugaseys must have had no problem if they'd needed to bribe someone at the consulate in Budapest. They all said goodbye with the one word they knew in a common language, "Shalom!"

Sailing on the Caribbean gave the family a taste of what it is like to live in the tropics. The heat and humidity would have been unbearable if they didn't have the breeze created by the moving ship. At the end of the second day out of Havana, they stopped in the port of Colon in the Panama Canal Zone to take on cargo. The next morning, they cruised through the amazing feat of engineering that connects the Caribbean to the Pacific. The heat was unbearable, since the ship went very slowly.

When they left the isthmus behind, they started to grow excited. Their next stop was Salinas, Ecuador!

What a shock awaited them two days later when Captain Venegas informed them that he was dropping anchor. There was no wharf, no gangplank!

They looked over the railing and saw a small boat pulled up close to the *Pacha Mama*. A sailor threw a rope ladder over the rail and climbed down with one of their suitcases on his shoulder. Other sailors followed, each carrying a suitcase.

Selma almost had to be pushed out of the freighter, she was so scared! But the sailors had been in this situation before and knew how to help a frightened matron from one ship to another on a rope ladder. The rest of the family followed. Captain Venegas waved and shouted, "Bienvenidos al Ecuador! Buena suerte a todos!"

Salinas was nothing more than a fishing village with houses and buildings made of split bamboo. How were they to get to Riobamba, the name of a place that Señor Zorer had written on their documents? They sat on their suitcases and ate some bananas as Abie changed some dollars into Ecuadorian coins at a shack with a sign on it "Banco de Fomento."

One of the *Pacha Mama* sailors who came ashore with them appeared. He motioned for them to follow him. They walked a few blocks and came to a building that seemed to be some sort of streetcar stop. The sailor waved them aboard the single car on the narrow track, the autocarril. Apparently, he had been sent ashore to be their guide.

The autocarril was filled with Ecuadorian men and women, all carrying packages in burlap sacks. The tram went through sandy fields with trees and plants that no one recognized. The tram went fast enough to create a breeze. The Europeans knew that Ecuador was a mountainous country and were wearing woolen clothes. They forgot that they'd be entering at sea level, almost exactly at the equator. What heat! What humidity! Much worse than Havana or Colon!

After an hour, the train screeched to a jolting stop. "Guayaquil! Guayaquil! Guayaquil!" the conductor shouted.

The Ecuadorians pushed past each other and piled out with their bundles. The nervous and polite Europeans were last to disembark with their luggage. They looked around, confused. Where to go next? The sailor had disappeared.

A man stepped forward. He looked like a European. He approached the family, smiling.

"I am Joachim List," he said in German.

The family was amazed and relieved.

"I am a representative of the Jewish community of Guayaquil. I have a manifest from every boat that carries refugees. I come here when I know that we will be having new arrivals. Willkomen im Ecuador!"

Señor List shook hands with everyone and pinched Enrique's cheek. "Come with me. All of our new arrivals stay at the boarding house on Boyaca Street for a few days until they find their new home."

The pension on Boyaca Street was only a few blocks away, but the family was nearly fainting from the heat. Wherever their new home was to be, it would NOT be on the steamy coast! They decided to stay only a few days in Guayaquil; they were anxious to get to Riobamba, wherever it was.

In those few days, the Cohens and Sauers received numerous visits from Jews who had come to Ecuador before them. Most of them had worked in agriculture for at least three years before leaving the countryside for the busy city of Guayaquil. Some were from Germany, but none from Aurich or Tauhaubischelstein. They came from Poland, Austria, France, Rumania, Ukraine. Ecuador was their port in a stormy world for Jews.

The family looked forward to going to Riobamba. They learned that it is the capital of Chimborazo Province. It was in the Andes, which everyone called the Sierra. A snow-capped volcano called Chimborazo overlooked the town, they were told. The Cohens pictured the alpine cities in Switzerland, with their quaint architecture and green valleys in the summer. Perhaps there were vineyards there, like in the northern part of Italy near the Alps?

The only way to get there, Señor List told them, was to take another train. That train terminal was on the opposite bank of the Guayas River, in Duran. As the dawn was breaking on a sweltering-hot morning, he accompanied them down to the Malecon boardwalk and helped them buy tickets for the ferry boat. Señor List waved to them as the train – hardly larger than the autocarril that had carried the family to Guayaquil from Salinas – pulled out. Señor List shouted, "Buena suerte!" Would they ever see him again?

Travellers crowded the train, carrying sacks of fruit and crates of groceries. In the back, a man put a wooden crate on the seat next to him that was full of ice to chill the shrimp he was taking to market. An Indian, wearing white pants and shirt, a black fedora hat and a heavy blue poncho carried a bundle of more ponchos with many colors and patterns. The air inside the train car was stifling and the windows would only open part-way. The Ecuadorian passengers stared at the strange family.

The train zigzagged up the mountain, barely clinging to the track. As they climbed the mountains, the family noticed the plants changing from tropical palms and rice fields to eucalyptus trees and corn plots and dairy cows. The houses changed, too. Bamboo was the common building material on the coast. The peasant homes in the higher altitudes were adobe brick covered with stucco.

After seven hours, they reached the Andean plateau.

It was freezing in the thin atmosphere, despite a nearly cloudless sky. At this altitude in Germany, there would be piles of snow everywhere. This was not Germany. This was not Italy. This was the Andes mountains in Ecuador.

There was snow on one place. To the east loomed the gigantic volcano Chimborazo with three snowy peaks. The wind that passed over its snow blew a chill onto all of the streets of Riobamba.

"Riobamba!" the conductor shouted, and waved to his passengers to get out.

One by one, the family members stepped off the train and looked around. When they were together with their suitcases, Herta looked at Abie and quietly asked, "What do we do now?"

PART FOUR

THE BOY'S MEMORIES

CHAPTER EIGHTEEN

LIFE IN RIOBAMBA

My earliest memories start when I was around three years old. The first thing I remember is standing outside of our little house with my Mami and Oma as my Papi rode away on a horse. At that time, I didn't know where he was going. I do remember that I was sadder about saying goodbye to the horse than to my Papi. The horse's name was Yegua, which really is just the Spanish word for mare, a female horse.

Our house in Riobamba, where I lived until I was seven years old, was small and cold. I always had to wear a couple layers of clothes even when I was inside, just to keep warm. My favorite memories of living in Riobamba are not about our house, or even about the city of Riobamba itself. What brings a smile to my lips is remembering the times that my Papi put me in front of him on the saddle, and Yegua walking briskly through the streets and then into the countryside. We were on our way to the place where Papi worked for five years: Hacienda Ancholag.

Hacienda Ancholag belonged to Señor Hector Albornoz. His ancestors had been among the Spanish Conquistadors who helped Francisco Pizarro conquer the Inca Empire in the 1500s. In payment for their efforts, the king of Spain granted the Conquistadors large plots of land. The grants included the native people who lived on the land to work for the Conquistadors and their families as serfs. Even though the Ecuadorian government declared all of them free many years later, most stayed on the same land in the same miserable conditions. They felt that they were part of the land and they were reluctant to leave it.

The Albornoz family raised dairy cattle, sheep, and rye. Papi received part of his wages in rye grain that Mami and Oma gave to a miller for rye flour—and bread to sell! Señor Albornoz had children, but they were all grown up and most had moved into town. He enjoyed having me around now and then. He had one of his workers saddle up a little pony for me to ride when he and Papi were out in the pastures.

Papi loved being out in the pastures. He told me that it reminded him of the Alps where he used to ski when he was a college student. And he loved farming, too. It wasn't quite the same as the grapevines in Italy he told me about, and the farm where I was born, but he was out in the fresh air all the time. I remember him telling me, "Someday, we will have an hacienda like this!" From the pastures half-way up a mountain, we could look across the valley and see the city of Riobamba spread out across its floor. Directly across was the magnificent volcano Chimborazo scraping the sky on the valley's far side.

We slept in a corner of the barn with a small, cast-iron stove in the corner so that we wouldn't freeze at night. Our only light was a kerosene lamp. Papi told me stories from the Torah – although I didn't really know that at the time; I thought he was making them up – and taught me some Jiu-Jitsu, too!

But I only went to Hacienda Ancholag a few times. Mostly, I stayed in Riobamba. There was a small park near our house. It wasn't a park with swings or other things for children to play with, but we could run around and play tag or make-believe games. At first, Opa Max took me to the park and watched over me. By the time I was five, he felt that the park was a safe place and that I could be left there to play with the local children without him. I think he felt silly being the only man at the park when all of the other children had their mothers or nannies watching them.

Like all children in Riobamba, I didn't start school until first grade at age six. Mami told me that in Germany, children started in kindergarten at age five. She wanted me to start learning when I was five, too, but there was no public library in Riobamba. There were only two book stores in the city and neither of them had books for children. Mami and Oma were always busy cooking, cleaning or baking bread, so Opa Max became my teacher.

First, he taught me the alphabet and my numbers. Then, he translated fairy tales that he remembered from his childhood, wrote them down, and then we would read them together. I think this helped Opa Max learn Spanish more than it helped me learn to read!

Opa Max was pretty lonely in Riobamba. He and Oma lost everything they'd built in Germany. He'd been an important businessman there. Now, he had very little to keep himself busy. He was too old to work in farming like Papi. Mami and Oma were busy with the house and baking bread. There were very few other Jewish refugees from Germany living nearby in Riobamba and Opa's Spanish was not good enough for him to have meaningful conversations with anyone outside of the family. The bookstores didn't sell books or newspapers in German. And he was too old-fashioned to consider baby-sitting for me as something a man of his age and education should do. He itched to get back into business. His time would come later!

When I turned six, it was time for me to start school. In Riobamba, there were three kinds of schools: The pious Catholic families sent their children to schools attached to churches where they were taught by nuns. Other Catholic families sent their children to private schools which cost quite a bit of money, but they knew that their children would make good connections there with children from their own class of society. Then there were the public schools. Many of them only went through third grade because the families who sent their children there were generally poor and the children were expected to start working after third grade.

My family was poor, so I went to a public school, Isabel Grameson. Isabel Grameson was the first woman of European blood to travel the entire length of the Amazon River and survive. There was one other Jewish pupil in my school. The Isaacovici family had come from Romania. Salamon Isaacovici was in third grade already and had his own friends, so he paid little attention to me.

I hated first grade. I already knew how to add and subtract numbers. I could read a little already. Opa had even taught me how to write my name and simple words. Most of the other children had never held a book in their hands before. None of my friends from the park were in this school.

My classmates looked at me with curiosity. Their parents were mostly mestizos, people who were part Indian and part European, but they were all very poor. Some of them still wore the traditional clothes of the Indian tribes who lived in villages near Riobamba.

Most of the students still lived in those villages and had to ride a public bus to come to Isabel Grameson School. Their mothers came with them on the bus. Most of the mothers worked as maids in the houses of families who sent their children to the other schools. Opa walked me to school and everyone treated us like we were from another planet. They were too shy or too scared to try to talk to me.

My teacher had gone to school only through the eighth grade. She had no idea of how to teach someone like me! I was bored and looked forward to when school ended at noon so that I could go home and learn with Opa Max.

A couple times a year, we would cram into the small home of another Jewish family in Riobamba, the Baiers, for dinner. Sometimes the Isaacovicis joined us. I didn't realize it at the time, but the reason we were eating together was because it was a Jewish holiday. I don't remember if we had anything like matzo at Passover or apples and honey at Rosh HaShana. I remember that the grownups sang songs, but whether they were German songs or Hebrew songs was a mystery to me at four or five years old. What I remember is that everyone was very happy, and that made me happy, too.

Just about the time I was to enter third grade, Papi came home with a big envelope in his hand. He waved it around and jumped up and down with excitement. The grownups all seemed to know what the paper was, but I just stood there jumping up and down like Papi because it was fun.

The reason everyone was so happy was that the paper was a letter from the Ministry of Immigration and Foreign Residents:

Congratulations! This is to document that the following persons
> Abraham Cohen
> Herta Sauer de Cohen
> Enrique Cohen Sauer
> Max Sauer
> Selma de Sauer

have successfully completed five years of residence in Riobamba, Ecuador. During this period, these persons have been supported by working in agriculture, as attested by Sr. Hector Albornoz. They have not become dependent on the Republic of Ecuador for maintaining their life and have abided by all of the laws of the Republic.

Therefore, according to the Terms of Immigration to which they agreed in 1939, they are free to leave Riobamba at their discretion and settle in a location of their choice in Ecuador or to leave this Country with no financial penalty. Should the persons named above wish to apply for citizenship in the Republic of Ecuador, they will be eligible for that status in 7 years.

Viva la Patria.

Signed, this 19ᵗʰ day June of 1944 in Quito,

Manuel Paredes Lasso,
Director General of Immigration and Foreign Residents

The next thing that Papi did shocked me!

He went into the bedroom that he shared with Mami and brought out a cloth bag. He opened the bag on the table where we ate all of our meals, and out poured dozens of coins, pieces of gold jewelry, and lots of paper money! I couldn't believe my eyes: never in all my seven years had I seen so much money, and I never imagined that poor people like us had so much money and gold!

After a moment, my mind changed from amazement to anger. Why had they been hoarding all of this money? Why hadn't they spent it on a better house or to send me to a school where I wouldn't be bored?

Papi could see on my face what my mind was thinking. He turned to me and pointing to the treasure on the table said, "Enrique, this is your future!"

I was even more confused. "My future? I didn't earn any of this money."

All the grownups laughed.

"No," Papi said. "This money is for us all to move to Quito. We are going to open a store there. We are going to send you to a better school there. And some day we will pay for you to go to a good university."

It never entered my mind that we'd ever leave Riobamba, much less move to Quito. The World War was still raging, so going back to Germany or even Italy was not possible for them. The United States was not accepting people born in Europe to immigrate there. The grownups all realized that their future – and mine – would be in Ecuador.

CHAPTER NINETEEN

LIFE IN QUITO

For the next few weeks, I saw little of Papi and Opa Max. They went to Quito, but I had no idea of what they were doing there. I supposed that the grownups didn't think that a little kid like me could understand the big changes in our life, nor did they think to ask me what I'd like to do in Quito. What I really wanted in Quito was to go to a better school where I wouldn't be bored.

Señor Albornoz helped us make the move to Quito. He had a pickup truck that he used to take big aluminum containers of milk from the hacienda into the creamery in Riobamba. He made a special trip into town this time and our family loaded our few possessions into the back of his truck. Mami and Oma got into the front of the truck with him. Papi, Opa and I sat on some blankets in the back to cushion the floor of the truck for what turned out to be a hard and bumpy ride.

The wind blew down cold from the snowy peaks of Chimborazo as we left Riobamba behind us. There was no one to see us off. As cold as it was, the trip was beautiful. The day was cloudless and the road from Riobamba to Quito was, as it is today, lined with many snow-capped volcanoes. Near the city of Ambato was the Tungurahua volcano, with smoke billowing out of the top of its snowy cone; just south of Latacunga was the giant Cotopaxi volcano that we could see from miles and miles away. Before we reached Quito, there were the twin volcanoes Ilinizas – the tall north peak and the smaller south peak.

The road was only one lane wide. At one point it had been paved, but now it was just full of holes. We were glad that we had the blankets each time the truck bumped through another one! Busses passed us and we passed busses. They were full of people from all across the Sierra – the highlands area – wearing their native costumes. The roofs of the busses were loaded with sacks of potatoes and all kinds of vegetables that the bus-riders were taking to the markets of Quito. There were chickens and ducks, too, flapping their wings to try and escape, even though their feet were tied to the bus.

At each town, we had to stop at least once because of the traffic. And when we stopped, we were immediately mobbed by local people trying to sell us food: fruits from Ecuador's coast like bananas and mangoes; favorite Ecuadorian dishes like roasted pork and shrimp cebiche. Mami had made us sandwiches and brought bottled water to drink. The food being sold was often covered with dust brought in on trucks like ours and wasn't really safe to eat. I felt sorry for the people who begged us to buy something. They all looked so poor, much poorer than us!

We approached Quito from the south. I was amazed. I'd never seen a city so large, even though Quito's population at that time was only about 100,000. The houses and churches stretched as far as the eye could see in the valley between Ecuador's two ranges of the Andes. As we drove closer to the center of the city, we passed a large hill, sitting all by itself on the valley floor: the Panecillo – Spanish for bread loaf. It made me think that I'd like to climb it one day to get a better view of everything I was seeing from the road.

We drove into the center of town with its narrow, cobble-stoned streets, winding up and down the sides of Pichincha volcano that forms Quito's western edge. There were pretty plazas with fountains every few blocks. Many people didn't have water in their houses back then and got their water from these fountains.

We had running water in our house. It was smack dab in the middle of downtown Quito, an area called "Quito Colonial" since most of the buildings – including our house – were built during the early Spanish colonial times in the 1600s and 1700s.

Our house was really an apartment. At one time, there had been one big house, but now it was broken up for three families to live in. Like almost all of the houses in Quito Colonial, we entered through a courtyard off the street. Often, there were small businesses that rented rooms on the street level. Our courtyard had pots of flowers all around the cobblestone patio. There was also a water faucet and a cement block for scrubbing clothes. The house had two stories and we lived on the second floor, with a balcony overlooking the patio. We had to walk a set of stairs to reach our apartment.

There were two large bedrooms: one for Mami and Papi and one for Oma and Opa. There was a tiny room – really meant for a servant – just big enough for a bed and a set of drawers. That was my bedroom. But I was so happy to have a room of my own! There was no window. The only windows were in the combined living room and kitchen and in the bigger bedrooms. There was an indoor toilet and a small bathtub, but no hot water anywhere. Still, it was still bigger and nicer than our place in Riobamba. I was glad that my parents had saved their money so that we could live in such luxury!

In no time at all, we'd settled in. The number one thing to do was to start making money! Papi and Opa had rented an empty store not far from the Sucre Theater, just a couple blocks from our house. We all pitched in to clean it up and put a fresh coat of paint on its 300-year-old walls.

Papi had learned some carpentry while working at Hacienda Ancholag and he set to work making shelves and display cases. Opa had beautiful handwriting and he painted a sign that announced to the neighborhood that this was "Nuevo Mercado Aleman" – the "New German Market." Something different, like being German, might bring in curious customers. Mami and Oma hired men to carry in big barrels that held things like sugar and rice and canned products that they put on the shelves. I was still too short to reach that high. My job was to go from house to house with flyers that announced our Grand Opening. It said:

**GRAND OPENING OF NUEVO MERCADO ALEMAN
NEXT TO THE SUCRE THEATER
BRING THIS FLYER TO GET A DISCOUNT
ON YOUR FIRST PURCHASE!**

I suggested that we give a free piece of candy to every child who came in with a parent. Everyone liked that idea.

"This boy already has a head for business!" Opa Max declared. It would be my job to give out the candy on Opening Day.

In reality, there wasn't much difference between our store and the other little markets in the neighborhood, except for one thing: Mami and Oma continued to bake their rye bread that had been so important in bringing money into our house in Riobamba. And it worked like a charm!

Shortly after the store opened, it was time for me to start school. I had hoped to go to a private school with a teacher who knew more than I did, but I was disappointed. Again, to save money until the store turned a profit, I was put into a public school, Escuela Espejo. It wasn't far from our house.

This was nothing like my school in Riobamba.

It was huge, three stories high! No one was as poor as my classmates in Riobamba. Most were children who lived in the neighborhood. Their parents worked in the shops and many worked for the City of Quito, since City Hall was just a few blocks away. Everyone was born in Quito like their parents and grandparents. Some even had ancestors whose names were inscribed on the wall of the Municipal Cathedral since they were among the founders of the city!

No question about it, however, I was an outsider. My classmates were cautious about making friends with me. I just didn't look right, and I spoke with an accent from Riobamba.

On the first day of class, my teacher, Señorita Aida, made me stand up and tell the class about myself. I was nervous!

"My name is Enrique Cohen Sauer," I said. Ecuadorians — like almost everyone in Latin America — use two last names: the father's comes first and then the mother's. "I was born in Italy and came to Ecuador when I was almost two years old. My family lived in Riobamba where my father worked on an hacienda and now we own the Nuevo Mercado Aleman."

"Italy!" I heard my classmates whisper between each other in amazement. They had rarely met anyone from outside of Quito, much less from Europe!

"Where does your family go to Mass?" asked a boy named Patricio.

"We don't go to Mass," I said, quietly, looking down at my shoes.

I heard a gasp go around the classroom. There were at least four Catholic churches within five blocks of our school. Just a few blocks in the other direction, near City Hall and the Presidential Plaza on the Plaza Grande, were the Municipal Cathedral and the Church of the Compania, with golden walls.

"Why don't you go to church?" Patricio asked politely.

"We are Jews. We don't go to church," I said softly. I couldn't tell them that Jews go to synagogue because I had never been a synagogue in my life. All I knew about being Jewish was that my Mami and Oma lit two candles and murmured a prayer I didn't understand on Friday nights when we had a nice dinner with two loaves of challah that they had baked earlier that day.

"Do you have any brothers or sisters?" another classmate asked. Just about every kid in my class in Riobamba had at least a half-dozen siblings, and I figured it was no different in Quito.

"No, it's just me," I said in a soft voice, getting more and more embarrassed, feeling more and more different.

That was the end of the questions. I think it was just too much for them to digest at one time: A strange boy from a strange country who had no other children in his family and didn't go to Mass.

CHAPTER TWENTY

CHANGES

Again, it was a lonely time for me. No one from my class invited me to play after school, so I spent most of my afternoons helping in the store or helping Oma with tasks around the house. What I liked best was hanging wet sheets out to dry on a clothesline we shared with the rest of the tenants in our courtyard. I made believe that the sheets were the sails of old ships and that I was the captain. If an imaginary pirate tried to board our ship, I would attack him with Jiu-Jitsu!

But most of the time, I was lonely. Finally, I spoke up at dinner one Sabbath evening. That was the only night that the store was closed and we ate together as a full family. Oma always lit two candles in heavy brass candlesticks.

"Papi, I need to tell you something important," I said. I'd rehearsed every possible answer to any questions or comments he might make. "I'm almost eight years old, but I don't have any friends here. No one wants to play with me because I'm a Jew."

"And what's wrong with being a Jew?" he asked.

"The priest has told them that the Jews killed Jesus. They believe that I killed Jesus! How could I do that when Jesus died hundreds of years ago?" I responded, angrily.

The grownups all shot looks at each other around the table. Oma sighed a deep sigh and covered her eyes. Then she spoke.

"I had hoped this would not happen here," she whispered, just loud enough for everyone to hear.

"That is a story, but not a true story, and people trust what the priest says as being the truth," Papi said, handing me a plate of roast chicken and potatoes. "I'm sorry that your classmates feel this way about Jews. The best thing you can do is be a good student and try to be kind and pleasant so that they will understand that Jews are good people. You must be an example to them about all Jewish people."

"But I don't know any other Jewish people except us and, the Isaacovicis and the Baiers!" I exclaimed. "I want to meet other Jews and I want to meet Jewish children like me!"

"The boy is right," Mami chimed in. "Maybe Opa will take Enrique to meet some other Jewish children next week after school."

Opa nodded. He liked to spend time with me.

"You mean there are other Jewish children in Quito?" I asked, hardly able to believe what Mami was saying. "You mean we're not alone, like in Riobamba?"

Mami smiled and shook her head. "No, there are quite a few Jewish children here. They just don't live in this neighborhood and they go to schools near their own homes."

My mind could hardly contain these facts. How did Mami know about these children? Why didn't she talk about them before? My rehearsed questions and answers didn't include this possibility, so all I could do was ask: WHEN?

Mami looked at Opa. "When do you want to take him?"

Opa was the person with the least responsibilities at home and at the store. He spent a good amount of time reading. Now that we were in Quito, there were several bookstores with books in German for sale. Little did I know, but the biggest chain of bookstores in all of Ecuador was owned by a Jewish refugee family who left Europe for Ecuador several years before I was born.

"How about Wednesday?" he asked me. "We will go right after you come home from school and have lunch."

I was overcome with excitement and couldn't even speak! I just nodded my head vigorously and everyone laughed.

The next few days I lived in a fog. All I could think about was going someplace where there were other Jewish children. Would they look like me or would they look like Ecuadorian children in my school?

Where did they live? What did their parents do? When did they come to Ecuador or were they born here?

Wednesday came and school could not end soon enough. The church bells around us rang twelve and I dashed out of the classroom and through the streets. I flew with wings on my heels to our house. Opa was waiting for me and so was the rest of the family. Most stores and businesses close in Quito from noon until two for siesta. Mami often kept the store open, but today they closed it at noon, too, so that they could see me off on what was, for me, an adventure as big as moving from Riobamba to Quito.

After a special lunch that Oma had prepared for this special occasion, and which I barely touched for being too excited, Opa and I bid them "hasta luego!" and set out to the main street in our part of town, Diez de Agosto. We caught a bus there, heading north along the length of the valley. I had only been on a bus a couple times, and we had always taken this bus. Before this trip, we had stopped at one of Quito's historic parks, El Alameda. It has a gigantic statue dedicated to heroes of Ecuador's independence and an Observatory. It also has room for kids to run around safely. But we didn't stop at the Alameda this time.

The Diez de Agosto took us through another part of town with more modern buildings and another, huge park, the Ejido, where we got off. The Ejido didn't have an observatory, but was full of huge trees and fountains that I could see from the street. We caught another bus that went east – to another part of town I'd never seen before. It was nothing like Quito Colonial. There were streets and streets of nice houses, tucked behind walls for safety and privacy.

Finally, we reached our destination. There was a sign: Colegio Americano. There was a beautiful school building with a large playground next to it. Children of all ages were playing soccer or other games. They seemed to be in small groups, but with boys and girls together.

"Is this the place, Opa?" I asked. "Is this where Jewish children go to school? Why doesn't it say Colegio Judio?"

Opa laughed, but his eyes were sad. I knew he realized how small my world was and felt sorry for me.

"There is no Jewish school for teaching subjects like arithmetic, or science, or world history," he explained, "but this school is run by people from the United States of America. Many Jewish families send their children here because they want their children to learn English. That way, it will be easier for them if they go and live or study in the United States someday."

"Can I go to school here, too?" I'd never thought of going anywhere except to the beach towns of Ecuador or to Europe to see where my family had lived before coming to Ecuador. "Maybe I'd like to go to the United States like them!"

Opa shook his head. "Enough talk! Let's go over meet some Jewish children!"

The gate to the playground was open, and we walked in. Opa and I walked over to where a teacher was standing.

Opa said to her, "I am Max Sauer. This is my grandson. We are new to Quito. We lived in Riobamba for five years. We are Jews. I understand that there are many Jewish children here. It would be very kind of you to let him play with them from time to time, even though he is not enrolled at Colegio Americano."

This was a BIG struggle for Opa. He still was having problems expressing himself in Spanish and had a heavy German accent.

The teacher looked at me kindly. "What is your name, young man?"

"Enrique Cohen!" I said proudly.

She nodded her head and turned to the playground, "Luis Liberman! Leon Pienknagura! Come over here, please!"

Two boys around my age broke away from their groups and came running to the teacher's side.

"Lucho, Leon. This is Enrique Cohen. He is new to Quito and lived in Riobamba. He is looking for some children to play with. Please be welcoming to him and introduce him to your friends."

The two boys offered to shake hands with me.

"Cohen?" Lucho (that's a Spanish nickname for Luis) said. "Are you Jewish?"

I was so petrified of saying something stupid. Even though the whole reason I was there was to meet other Jewish children, I couldn't speak.

Opa answered for me, "Yes, we are Jews. We came from Europe about five years ago."

"Oh, where in Europe?" Leon asked.

"Why do you ask?" inquired the teacher.

"Because that is how we make our teams. There's a German team, a Polish one, an Austrian one. There's one from Italy and others from Rumania, Holland, and Belgium. You can play on the team that has kids from your country," Leon explained.

"I was born in Italy," I said, happy to hear that there was someone else whose family was Italian.

"Come on, then," Lucho said, grabbing my wrist. "I'll introduce you to the Ottolenghi kids."

The four Ottolenghi children were huddled together with three or four other children. Lucho brought me over to their circle and said, "This is Enrique Cohen. He's new to Quito. He was born in Italy, so he goes on your team." And with this introduction, he turned and ran back to his Rumanian team.

"My name is Abraham Ottolenghi," the oldest boy said, in a strange language, and then seemed to introduce the rest of the team.

I was confused and embarrassed. I thought they'd be speaking in Spanish!

"I'm sorry, I don't understand you," I said in Spanish. "Are you speaking English or Italian?"

"Why, Italian, of course," Abraham replied in Spanish. "When we're together in teams, we always speak our mother tongue. So do the other teams."

"I see," I continued, "but I wasn't even two years old when we arrived in Ecuador and we only speak Spanish at home."

"Don't your parents speak Italian?"

"They can, I suppose. They lived there for a few years before I was born, but they were born in Germany."

"Well, then, do you speak German?"

"No. We only speak Spanish."

The Italians turned their backs and had a short conference.

"Okay, you can be on our team, but we're not going to speak Spanish just because you don't speak Italian," Abraham said with a sigh. "The two languages are pretty close. Listen well and you'll catch on."

And so it was. Every Wednesday afternoon, Opa and I would get on the bus on the Diez de Agosto and ride to Colegio Americano. Sometimes, I'd play soccer with the Italians. Sometimes I'd play with the Germans. I became a really good player because sometimes I'd surprise people with some Jiu-Jitsu moves that Papi had taught me. I was able to combine them with soccer moves and score a goal. When I started doing that, I became pretty popular and teams from other countries wanted me. In that way, I got to meet a lot of kids, but since I never played regularly with any particular team, I really didn't make any good friends.

The only thing that distinguished these Jewish players from the Ecuadorian players at Colegio Americano was that many of them wore a Jewish star dangling from their neck. Oma wore a Jewish star on Friday nights at our Sabbath dinner. Until I played soccer with Jewish boys, I didn't know that boys could wear them, too. I started learning a little about how Jews acted a little differently than other kids.

CHAPTER TWENTY-ONE

A SHOCKING SURPRISE

I wouldn't say I was completely happy with how my life was, but it was okay. My teachers at Colegio Espejo tried to give me homework that was a bit harder than what many of the other students got. They knew that I wanted to learn more and that my parents and grandparents were well-educated and could help me if I needed it.

I was just eleven years old and working on my homework in the little storeroom at the back of the store when a strange man came in. He wore a nice suit and hat and carried a briefcase with a red cross on a white background with him. The minute the grown-ups noticed him, they all stopped what they were doing and walked toward the door together. I peeked out of the doorway to see what was happening.

"Does this store belong to Señor Abraham Cohen?" the man asked in Spanish.

"I am Abraham Cohen," Papi replied, and offered his hand to the stranger. After they shook hands, Papi grabbed Mami's hand. I'd never seen him do anything like that before in public.

"Señor Cohen," the man continued. "As you can see, I'm here from the Red Cross here in Quito. My name is Cristobal Padilla. We have received a telegram from our international headquarters in Switzerland. We are trying to contact all German men around the world named Abraham Cohen to determine which is the one who was born in Aurich, Germany in 1910."

"And why do you want to know this?" Papi looked scared; he could barely look at Señor Padilla in the eye. I knew that Papi had killed a man in self-defense in Aurich. As I think back on it, I imagine he thought that this might be someone who was actually from the German police, searching to arrest him for murdering that policeman so many years ago.

"I am here to tell Abraham Cohen from Aurich that his mother is still alive," the man answered. "What is your mother's name?"

"Her name is Jette Cohen," Papi replied.

Señor Padilla took a deep breath. "Your mother is alive, señor."

And then Papi fainted. Right there in the middle of the **store**. In front of everyone.

Mami ran to the back of the store to get a bottle of water and I ran with her to give it to Papi. Opa and Señor Padilla pulled Papi up onto a chair that Oma grabbed from behind the counter.

Papi took a while to be able to talk. His first words were, "My mother is alive!" He was shaking all over. He looked at me and said, "My mother is alive!" It was like he was a little boy, so excited!

Señor Padilla told us that she had survived the horrors of Auschwitz. Her husband had died there, but didn't know if any of her children had survived.

"Where is she?" Papi asked, still trembling from the shock. "Is she in Ecuador?"

Señor Padilla laughed. "No, no. She and her husband are in the United States. In Ohio," he explained.

"Her husband? I thought my father died!" Papi gasped.

"Your father died very shortly after arriving at the concentration camp, I'm sorry to say," Señor Padilla continued. "In the camp, she met another man, Jerome Oberlin. They were married in a displaced persons camp after liberation. He has relatives in Ohio who sponsored them to come to the United States. Her name now is Jette Oberlin. Here," he said, handing Papi a large envelope, "this is a transcript of a letter she has written to you, telling you about her life and situation."

Papi took the envelope, but gave it to Mami. His hands were too shaky still.

Señor Padilla reached into his brief case and took out some business cards.

"If you don't hear from me again soon, please feel free to call me or stop at our office. We aren't far from City Hall, on an upper floor."

"*Que Dios le pague*, God will reward you," said Mami, which is what Ecuadorians say when they want to let people know that they are truly grateful for a kind deed. "This is our son, Enrique. We have never talked to him about Abraham's parents. It has been too painful. Now, we can tell him about her and maybe someday he will meet her."

Mami didn't know how soon that day would come.

CHAPTER TWENTY-TWO

NEW PLACES

Papi read the letter out loud, but it was in German, so I didn't understand a thing. Every now and then he would stop reading because whatever he read was making him cry. That made Mami cry, and soon all of the grownups were crying. These were NOT tears of happiness. I felt that I could wait to learn what was in the letter because I didn't want them to cry even more.

"Are you going to write a letter to Oma Jette in Ohio?" I asked. "I'd like to write to her, too!"

"Yes, yes," Papi answered, smiling at my kind gesture, "but Oma Jette doesn't read Spanish. You can tell me what you want to write and I'll translate it into German."

That night, in my windowless bedroom, I sat on my bed and used the little dresser to write a letter in Spanish to a grandmother I'd never met and knew absolutely nothing about except what Señor Padilla had said in the store.

Dear Oma Jette,

> *My name is Enrique Cohen, but when I was born in Italy, my name was Enrico. I am your grandson. Abraham Cohen is my father and Herta Sauer de Cohen is my mother. We live in Quito, Ecuador now. I go to Escuela Espejo and I think I'm a good student. I like to play soccer once a week with Jewish boys and girls who go to Colegio Americano.*

I am sorry that my grandfather died. I am happy that you have a new husband. Do you like living in Ohio? I like Ecuador but I would like to go to Ohio someday to meet you and give you a hug. Would you like to come visit us in Quito?

That's all I can say right now. I am happy that you are alive. My Papi is very happy, too.

Sincerely,
Enrique Cohen

After the store closed the next day, Papi and I sat down together. We hadn't really had time together like this since the last time he took me to Hacienda Ancholag. Papi translated the letter that his mother had written in German into Spanish for me and translated my letter into German for her.

Hearing Oma Jette's words, I understood why everyone cried when Papi first read her letter. It was mostly a list of Papi's friends and relatives from Aurich who had died. She explained how she and her new husband had met and how they ended up in Toledo, Ohio. There was no picture of her with the letter and I tried hard to imagine what she might look like. Papi and I look quite a bit alike, so I thought we must look like his dead father, too. But his mother?

Papi read my letter and smiled. "I think she will like this letter from you very much. She needs to know that you are having a good life. She had so little to be happy about for a long time."

The next day, we walked together to the Plaza Grande. A man was there who took pictures of people standing in front of the Independence Monument. Papi paid him to take a picture of me and while he went into a small store on the plaza to develop it, Papi and I went to the post office to buy stamps. When the picture was developed, we put it in the big envelope with our letters and gave it to a post office clerk.

"How long should this letter take to arrive in the United States?" Papi asked the clerk.

"Hmm," the clerk looked at the address, "it's going to Ohio." He took out a map of the United States from under the counter. "If the letter goes on a ship that's going to Los Angeles or San Francisco in

California, it'll take about two weeks. And then another three or four days from there to Ohio." He pointed to Ohio near the middle of the country.

"That's too long!" I shouted. "My abuelita is an old woman. She could die before it arrives!"

The clerk laughed. "That's the *short* route. If the boat is headed to New Orleans or Miami or even New York City, it has to go through the Panama Canal and it will take even longer."

"Don't worry, Enrique," Papi assured me. "Your Oma Jette is a strong woman, even if she seems old to you. She'll live to get your letter."

I was satisfied with the answer and we headed home. I couldn't wait to tell my Jewish friends that I have another grandmother and that she's in the United States.

When Opa and I got to Colegio Americano on Wednesday, the other kids didn't seem that interested. Just about all of them had relatives somewhere in America. Many of them were planning to move to the United States after their fathers had completed their five years of work service. What was more interesting to them was something on my back.

I'd taken off my shirt because I was getting too hot and only wore a sleeveless tee shirt.

"What's THAT?" Elio Schachter asked, in a voice dripping with disgust.

"I can't see! It's on my back," I answered, trying to feel for what Elio saw.

"Caramba! I've never seen anything like it!" Herbert Max added.

I wasn't going to take any more nasty insults about my back without knowing what it was. I ran over to where Opa was sitting on a bench, reading a book in German.

"Opa!" I cried, running over to get his attention. He looked up. "Opa, the kids are making fun of me. They say I've got something disgusting on my back!"

Opa turned me around and I looked over my shoulder at him. He wrinkled up his nose and touched a spot just above my shoulder blades. Yow! It was sensitive!

"What's there?" I demanded to know.

"It looks like a boil. I haven't seen anyone with a boil in years. Nasty things they are!"

"Is it infectious?" I asked. I didn't want to pass it on to the kids on my team.

"No," Opa laughed. "But it must be taken care of properly so that it doesn't get worse for you."

"Let's go home and see if Mami or Oma can do anything. I want to get rid of this NOW!"

Mami was home by the time we reached there and took a look at my back.

"It's ugly, that's for sure," she said, shaking her head. "Wait here at the kitchen table."

She left the room and came back in a minute with her sewing basket and pulled out a long needle. I knew what she was going to do. Just like when I'd get a wood splinter in my finger, she'd pass the needle through a flame to sterilize it and then use it to poke out the splinter. So she did in this case, piercing the ugly boil until it oozed nasty, bloody pus. And it hurt! She put some alcohol on it and covered it with a clean bandage.

"I hope that does it," she sighed.

It didn't. Within a couple days, there were more boils on my back. We had no choice but to go to a clinic and see a doctor. I'd only been to a doctor's office a couple times for school vaccinations. I was a healthy kid.

The clinic of Dr. Sotomayor was just a few blocks away and Mami took me there right after school. Dr. Sotomayor took one look at my back and, like Mami, shook his head.

"This is the worst case of boils I've ever seen!" he exclaimed. "I can prescribe a lotion, but there's no guarantee that it will help such a bad case."

He was right. The lotion was useless and the boils continued to spread. We went back to Dr. Sotomayor after a week.

"I think that the lotion didn't work because our air here in Quito is so very dry. It would help, I think, if you took him somewhere with more humid air and where his skin can get lots of moisture." Mami and I looked at each other and we both shrugged. He continued. "My brother-in-law owns a spa in Baños with thermal baths. I will give you a letter of introduction and you should spend a good month there. I'll give you instructions, too, about how to care for his skin after each bath."

Mami's face showed mixed emotions. She was happy that there was a possible cure, but worried about how much it would cost. She took the letter and the instructions, and thanking him politely, put her hand on my shoulder and walked me out the door.

"Am I going to Baños?" I asked with excitement. I'd heard about this town at the edge of the jungle, with pools that got their heat from the molten interior of the Tungurahua volcano. The jungle! What an adventure!

"We will get there somehow."

I went about my life as usual for a couple days. I knew how worried Mami was about the expense of staying in Baños for a whole month. But Mami was not a woman to let others make decisions for her. While I was in class or helping Oma around the house, she was out making preparations. One morning, when I went to take my place at the kitchen table, I found three suitcases waiting by the living room door.

I looked at her, calmly drinking her coffee. She was not wearing the apron she always put on before heading out for the store. She read my mind.

"Yes, Enrique, we are leaving for Baños after breakfast," she said.

"What about school today?"

"In that suitcase," she pointed to a large bag, "are all your books and all your assignments for the next month. Your teacher was very helpful. Señora Aida wants you to get well, too."

"What about the store?"

"Opa is going to have to do more. Remember, he had a big business in Germany. He knows how to do the book-keeping better than I do!"

"What about my clothes? I didn't pack anything in a suitcase!"

"We are not taking much clothing from Quito. It is much warmer in Baños. We shall buy lighter shirts for you, and even some swimming trunks for when you sit in the baths."

Mami hadn't missed a trick. She never did.

Papi, Oma and Opa were waiting for us on the patio downstairs. Papi stepped out and hailed a taxi cab from the Diez de Agosto. A taxi cab! I'd never been in one in my life! But our suitcases were too many and too heavy to carry on a bus to wherever we were going. Oma and Opa hugged me. Papi put the bags in the trunk of the taxi and then shook my hand.

"You must take good care of Mami when you are in Baños," he advised, sternly. "Make sure that she is not lonely or sad. That is your job while you are there…and of course, your school work!"

As Mami and I got into the back seat of the cab, Papi gave the driver instructions, "To the Cumanda!" and paid him in advance.

I was too excited to cry upon leaving my family.

The Cumanda was Quito's bus terminal, but there was no building. The Cumanda was in a small bowl-shaped valley on the south side of town. There were dozens of small booths spread around it; each was the "office" for a different bus company. The FBI – Flota Babahoyo Interprovincial – went to the coast. The CIA – Compania Interprovincial Ambato – went to Ambato and beyond into the new towns in the jungle (called the Oriente in Ecuador). The taxi driver left us off at the CIA booth and unloaded our luggage.

The Cumanda was full of action – and dust! Buses came and went with little attention to any people who might have stepped into their path. There were Indians from all over the country, each in the traditional costume of their particular tribe. People were selling all kinds of things for travellers to enjoy on their journey: bananas and mangoes, sweet biscuits, little cups of gelatin, toasted dried hominy corn, and little bags of salted chocho beans which were my favorite. I had brought a few coins of my own money and bought a bag of chochos to share with Mami.

Mami bought two tickets and the ticket-seller helped carry our suitcases into the bus. Mami would not let him put them on the bus's roof with all of the chickens and ducks in cages. There were burlap sacks of products from the northern part of Ecuador that would be sold in the markets at Baños and beyond. She wanted to keep a watchful eye on our precious cargo.

We climbed aboard and in no time at all, nearly every seat was full. I sat next to the window so that I wouldn't miss a glimpse of the new scenery I was anxious to see. The first part of the trip was familiar. We took the same road as we had used to move from Riobamba to

Quito. Once we reached Ambato, the road turned to the east and we headed toward Baños. The road was narrow and hugged the edge of the mountains. As we drove ever lower beyond the Andes, the countryside changed. Gone were the agave plants and eucalyptus trees of the Sierra. Now, there were banana trees in the yards of the houses along the road and the small villages we passed. Here and there, a waterfall drizzled its stream onto the roof of the bus (Mami was even happier now that we kept our bags inside). And there were flowers everywhere – even orchids growing wild!

It was late afternoon and I had nodded off with my head on Mami's shoulder when I awoke to hear the bus driver shout "Baños! Baños! Baños!" Everyone rushed to get off the bus first, but Mami and I waited until everyone was gone to drag our bags to the front. As the bus driver helped us with our luggage, Mami pulled out Dr. Sotomayor's letter from her purse and showed it to him.

"Do you know where is the Hosteria San Luis here in Baños?"

The bus driver lifted an eyebrow. "San Luis?" he asked. "That is a beautiful hosteria!"

He called to a teenager lounging on the wooden sidewalk in front of a store, "Santiago! Come and help the gringos with their bags. They are going to Hosteria San Luis!"

I was surprised that he called us gringos. That was a term that my friends and I used when talking about Americans. I was an Ecuadorian. But, maybe, Mami and I looked like gringos to the bus driver.

Santiago didn't say a word. He was wearing a short-sleeved shirt, dirty cotton pants and sandals with no socks. I suddenly realized how warm it was in Baños, and pulled off the sweater I'd been wearing since leaving our house. Santiago grabbed the heaviest suitcase and jerked his head to indicate to Mami and me to follow him.

The streets in Baños were unpaved but there was little traffic. Most of the houses were of split bamboo with palm-thatched roofs. What made it beautiful, though, was the dense tropical vegetation. Everyone had banana or mango trees surrounding the house, protecting it from the hot sun. Most houses had porches where the family could sit together to take in the evening breeze. Pots of colorful flowers hung from the eaves or lined the edge of the porches. Santiago waved to everyone and they waved back. It was a friendly town. I liked it already.

After wandering for about five blocks, we stopped where the street ended. There was a high wall with a sign painted on it: Hosteria San Luis. Santiago shouted, "Open the gate! There are guests here for you!" He turned to face Mami who gave him a coin for carrying our bags and he left without another word.

A tall, handsome man dressed all in white came to the gate and opened it for us.

"Welcome to Hosteria San Luis," he said, smiling. "I am Pepe Vazquez. What brings you here?"

Again, Mami reached into her purse. This time she pulled out Dr. Sotomayor's letter and handed it to the man. He glanced at it quickly and said, "Ahhh! A patient of my brother-in-law! We will take special care of you! Come in! Leave your bags here. My boy will take care of them in a minute."

The house was made of brick and stucco with a red tile roof. There was a broad veranda surrounding it with comfortable-looking chairs and small tables scattered along it. Like the other homes in Baños, there were flowers and fruit trees everywhere. Inside, there were beautiful paintings of the Andes mountains on the plastered walls. The furniture was carved wood with colorful upholstery. I'd never been in such a luxurious house! Mami seemed very pleased with what she saw.

"Please sit down," Señor Pepe said, "I will ask my wife to bring you some refreshment."

And then he did something that really surprised us. He turned on a light switch! Although it was turning dark, we had not seen a single street light in Baños nor did we see any poles with wires leading to the houses for electricity. It was quiet in the house, but we could hear a hum coming from outside. Hosteria San Luis had its own electricity generator. What luxury on the edge of the jungle!

In a minute, a beautiful woman entered the room with a tray of naranjilla juice and some cookies. She was wearing the costume of the Salasacan Indian tribe: a short black wool skirt and a white blouse with puffy sleeves, all embroidered delicately. Señor Pepe followed her.

"May I introduce my wife, Rosa?" he said. I was shocked. I didn't expect a sophisticated man like Señor Pepe to be married to an Indian woman. "She is the one who made the paintings on the walls." He swept his arm dramatically around the room, bursting with pride at his wife's talent.

Everyone shook hands, as is the Ecuadorian custom.

After our snack, a young man came into the room, introduced himself as Victor, and asked us to follow him to our room. We followed him out to the veranda and walked until there was an open door: our room, our home for the next month. It had twin beds, a large dresser, a tall cabinet to hang clothes and jackets, a night-stand and — a bookshelf with books! Again, what luxury! Could we afford this?

Now, we started a routine that would last for a month. In the morning, we had breakfast with Señor Pepe and Señora Rosa. Then, Mami and I would walk around Baños to see what was new or to stop at the post office (just a big table in a general store, really) to send a letter to the family in Quito and buy a newspaper. After a heavy lunch, I'd soak in the warm, spring-fed pool during siesta while Mami read the newspaper out loud. In the late afternoon, I sat on the veranda and did my school work. We'd have a light dinner and then it was bedtime once Mami had put the medicine on my back.

We were the only guests at Hosteria San Luis during the weekdays, but on the weekends almost all of the rooms were taken by visitors from Quito or another city in the Sierra. There was only one kid on one weekend and she was just a little girl of three or so.

I'll never forget the first time I saw the pool. It was early on the morning after we arrived, as we were heading into the dining room for breakfast. I saw a thick mist rising from behind a hedge of hibiscus bushes. Mami and I went to investigate and there it was: a cement pond with steaming water flowing into it from a crack in a rock behind it along an open tiled pipe. Then, the water flowed out of the pool through a little lip on the pool's edge and into the garden.

When Mami first saw it, she laughed and said, "Ach! This reminds me of the mikveh in Tauber!"

"What's a mikveh?"

She giggled a bit. "It's a special bath for Jewish people. I went one time when I was about your age with my Oma Anna – that's Oma Selma's mother. She was very pious and went to the mikveh regularly. She wanted me to know what it was in case I ever wanted to go myself."

"So, did you ever go yourself?"

"Ach, no!" I found it interesting that Mami was using a bit of German while she was remembering this event from her past. "That is for the very religious Jews. *We* are modern Jews!"

So, little by little, I learned a bit more about how different kinds of Jews behave.

I don't know if it was the warm water of the hot springs in Baños, or if it was the lotion that Mami put on my back at night, or if it was the humid, sub-tropical sun and air that had such a healing effect on my back, but by the time a month passed, I had only one or two tiny boils still in the process of disappearing. It was time to go home.

We said a sad goodbye to Señor Pepe and Señora Rosa. Mami gave a great sigh as Victor closed the gate behind us and we followed him back to the bus stop on the main plaza in Baños. We boarded the CIA bus and retraced our route to Quito. As the bus climbed back into the cold, thin air of the Andes, I realized how I'd gotten used to the warm climate of Baños and how much I liked it.

It was late afternoon when we arrived in Quito. We took a taxi again, but this time it was to the store because we knew that the rest of the family would be there. There were a few regular customers there, too, and everyone greeted us warmly. When Oma hugged me, she pulled up the back of my shirt at the same time.

"Look, Max!" she exclaimed to Opa, and she spun me around. "His back is almost perfectly clear!"

Everyone gave a cheer! I felt like a hero. I had beaten the terrible boils! Or so I thought.

School had finished for the year already. It was time to say "adios" to Escuela Espejo and "hola" to a new one. Escuela Municipal Especial (everyone called it the EME) was totally new and with a new concept in education. It was for gifted and talented students. I was proud that I qualified to be admitted. My teacher at the Escuela Espejo, Señorita Aida, had recommended me to the principal.

I loved the EME. I was never bored. And I made real friends, especially Augusto Maldonado. In a short time, we were almost inseparable. I loved going to his house in a neighborhood near the Alameda Park. It was close enough for me to walk there, now that I was nearly twelve years old. We'd do our homework together, play basketball one-on-one, and spend what little money we had on ice cream and other treats.

But every Wednesday, I'd still go to Colegio Americano to play with the Jewish kids. When everyone was speaking Spanish together, I'd often catch words or phrases about Jewish activities, words like Bar Mitzvah or Yom Tov. I didn't want to look stupid and ask them what these were, but by the time I got home to ask Opa, I usually forgot what I was going to ask.

Life was good. Until the boils came back. The school year was more than half over. But the boils were worse than ever.

"This is it!" Mami announced to the family when the situation couldn't be ignored any longer. "Whatever cured him in Baños was not permanent. We must send Enrique to the United States to find a way to cure him once and for all!"

Papi nodded. "We must send him to Toledo. The American doctors will know how to treat him! And it will be a good thing for him to know his Oma Jette and her husband. He'll learn English, too."

No one seemed to care what I was thinking about this. Me, I wanted to go back to Baños and give it another try there.

Again, out came the bag that I knew held money and gold jewelry. Mami dumped its contents onto the table again. It's clear that our time in Baños had used up a good portion of the treasure. She scooped up most of the jewelry.

"Oma Selma and I have been carrying this jewelry around for a long time," Mami said, looking at me. "It's the last of what remains from our life in Germany. But we will use it for you to have a healthy life in Ohio."

I didn't know if I should cry or if I should feel guilty. My family was willing to make big financial sacrifices for me. That meant they must love me, even though they never said it out loud. But all I had done was waste it on useless cures, even though I had no control over the boils.

With all their sacrifices, why did I feel angry that I wanted to stay in Ecuador? Was I so selfish?

I sat down, sad and resigned to my fate.

"When will I go?"

"As soon as I can arrange for a passport and airfare," Mami replied.

"Airfare?" My ears perked up. "You want me to go to Toledo on an airplane?"

"Of course," Mami replied, as if it was the only natural response. "It will take weeks for you to get to Toledo on a boat and train. We want you in Ohio quickly. You are almost twelve and you are a very responsible young man now. You can do it."

"You mean I'm going to fly all the way to Toledo all by myself? You're not coming with me?" I shouted with fear and amazement.

"Of course. We cannot afford a second ticket."

And so it was. Just as she did for our trip to Baños, Mami set about with her German efficiency and arranged everything within a month. All I had to do was have a picture taken for my passport and go with her to the American embassy to sign the application for a visa.

Papi wrote several letters to Oma Jette during that month and sent them by *air mail* to make sure they arrived at her home quickly. She wrote back that she and Jerry (she called her husband Jerome by a nickname) would be glad to have me. She made it clear, though, that I might be a bit of a financial burden to them. Although the Cohen families in Toledo and Quito had lost everything in the war, we had yet to receive any reparations from the German government. Neither did the Sauers.

I tried to make the most out of every day at the EME and with Augusto. He was excited that I was going to America and made me promise to send postcards from the Grand Canyon and the Empire State Building.

My Jewish friends at Colegio Americano were curious. Toledo, Ohio? They'd never heard of it. All their relatives lived in places like Chicago or Saint Louis or New York City. Still, they wished me good luck and said that they'd miss having me on their teams.

PART FIVE

AMERICA

CHAPTER TWENTY-THREE

TRAVELLING ALONE

The day came for me to leave. It was one of those perfect Quito mornings. The sky was such a clear blue that you could see nearly every snow-capped mountain throughout the "Avenue of Volcanoes" from Quito. Only Mami came with me to the airport, although I'd hoped that Opa Max would come, too. He had tears in his eyes when we said goodbye at Nuevo Mercado Aleman. I think he was scared of losing me, the only grandson from his only daughter.

Mami gave me confidence to travel so far all by myself. She told me how she'd gone to Milan all by herself when she was only a little older than me. I think she was trying to convince herself that I would do all right by myself on this journey.

After we checked my suitcase, Mami tied a burlap bag with my name on it around my neck. Inside were all of the documents I needed to get to and enter the United States. There were a few American dollars in it. There also was a letter, written in German, to Oma Jette and Jerry, along with their telephone number in Toledo.

"Whatever you do, don't lose anything from that bag!" she warned me. "And only talk to the stewardess on the plane. No strangers!" With that, she gave me a fast hug, turned me around by my shoulders, and pushed me into the line of passengers waiting to board the Panagra flight to Chicago. I didn't dare look back, scared to see if she would walk away before I even boarded the plane.

I climbed the metal stairs to board the plane. A pretty woman in a uniform with a nametag that said "Angela" on it took my ticket. She said something in English. I shook my head.

Then, she said in Spanish, "Welcome aboard! I will be your special guide to Dallas. Someone else will guide you to Chicago."

Mami had taken care of everything.

Mami also arranged for me to have a window seat. She remembered how I wanted one on our bus ride to Baños.

Mami didn't say "I love you" but she showed how much she cared in different little ways, like this.

It was a long flight to our first stop in Dallas and we made several stops along the way to pick up and drop off other passengers and re-fuel. Flying over the Andes was beautiful, with farms and towns scattered between the mountains. Flying over the Gulf of Mexico was boring and after Angela served me lunch on a tray, I fell asleep until I felt her hand, shaking me gently on the shoulder.

"Wake up," she said, "we'll be landing in Dallas in about a half hour."

I was stiff from sitting so long. The boils on my back itched and ached from pressing against the seat back for hours. I was ready to get to Toledo and take a soothing, warm bath.

I saw Angela talking with another woman in the same uniform at the exit. The two walked over to my seat.

"This is Marie," Angela said. Marie offered to shake hands. I liked her immediately. Angela continued, "My part of the flight is over now. Marie will take my place in helping you when you get to Chicago. But she doesn't speak Spanish. I know you'll get along just fine, though. I've explained everything to her."

"Mil gracias, Señorita Angela," I told her. "*Dios le pague.*"

The flight from Dallas to Chicago was exciting because I knew I was flying over America. It was boring because everything was flat, and a lot of it was dry and brown. The pilot made an announcement and I understood the word "Mississippi." I knew it was an important river from my Geography class. Looking out the window, I saw a big river and we followed it for much of the trip.

Another meal on a tray. Another uncomfortable nap. The sun had set by the time we landed in Chicago. I looked into the sky when I stepped off the plane with Marie next to me. The stars were not the stars I was used to seeing in Quito. I was a stranger in a strange land.

In the airport, everything was new and confusing. All the signs were in English. Everyone was talking in English, or some other language that I didn't know. The hallways in the airport seemed to go on forever. I held onto Marie's hand with all my might. I might have felt pretty grown-up at almost twelve years old in Quito, but I felt like a kindergartener in the Chicago airport.

Marie and I found my luggage easily. Mami had tied a ribbon with the colors of the Ecuadorian flag onto the handle. Then Marie took me into a long line where a man in a booth wearing a uniform looked at my passport and visa, and told us to pass along. We put my suitcase on a table where another man looked inside.

"Is he bringing in any plants or unwrapped food?" he asked Marie. She shook her head.

We passed through a set of doors and found ourselves in another long hallway. My brain was bursting with all these new sights, sounds, and smells. People at the airport were all dressed up in nice clothes for their trips in airplanes. I felt that my clothes were shabby compared to theirs.

At last, Marie and I passed through a set of large swinging doors and saw a huge crowd of people. Everyone was pushing to get to the front to see who would walk through the doors next. I wondered where my Oma Jette was. I didn't know what she looked like. The picture of me at the Plaza Grande was almost a year old and I'd grown a lot. Would she recognize me? Marie and I stood still, waiting.

Finally, when most of the crowd had disappeared, an elderly couple stepped forward. They were wearing shabby but neat clothes and their shoulders were stooped. The woman held a piece of cardboard in one hand. When she held it up, written in red crayon was one word: COHEN. This was Oma Jette and her husband! I looked up at Marie and pointed to the woman with the sign and then to myself.

"Gracias, Marie," I said, dropped her hand and ran to the open arms of Oma Jette.

She hugged me like I'd never been hugged before. Her husband hugged us both. Oma Jette started talking in German.

I looked at her and said in Spanish, "I don't speak German."

Her husband shook his head and said something in another language. English, I imagined. I shook my head again. This was going to be a tough start, I thought.

Oma looked at me, pointed to herself and said, "Oma Jette."

Okay, she wanted me to call her Oma Jette.

Her husband did the same and said, "Jerry."

I had a hard time pronouncing the J (Oma Jette's pronounced her name with a Y sound instead of a J) for Jerry, but I tried it with difficulty. Everyone laughed.

I pointed to myself and said, "Enrique."

We all repeated it and that's pretty much all I said for a couple days.

Even though it was dark, we headed into a parking lot and found an old gray car parked alone. Jerry put my suitcase in the trunk, opened the back door for me, and we headed off. I wondered if we were far from Toledo and how long it would take to drive there, but since I had no way to ask, I just waited to find out. Since it was dark, I saw nothing, but I could tell that there were no hills or mountains. Now and then, I dozed. Once or twice, we stopped at a gas station or café. I couldn't believe that Jerry didn't fall asleep at the wheel!

Shortly after dawn, Jerry honked the horn and shouted to get my attention. He pointed at a sign that said "Welcome to Toledo. The Glass City." When I looked at the clock on the car's dashboard, I saw that we'd be on the road for over eight hours!

My first impulse was to compare what I saw with what I knew. And Toledo was nothing like Quito or even Riobamba. The houses and buildings were of brick or wood, nothing like the white stucco buildings in every part of the Ecuadorian Sierra. There was a tidy lawn in front of each house and none of the houses had a wall around it. All the streets were paved and had wide sidewalks. There wasn't a palm or eucalyptus tree anywhere.

We drove into a neighborhood that looked a bit older than some of the others we'd passed through. The streets had trash in the gutters and many of the houses needed a new coat of paint. This wasn't how I imagined America. I'd seen pictures in magazines of luxurious houses with swimming pools in the back. These houses were *not* like that!

Jerry turned the car onto a street and pointed to the street sign: Vermont. Then he tapped his head to tell me to remember that name. It was easy to say "Vermont" because it's the same in Spanish as in English. Oma Jette clapped her hands when I said the word correctly. Whew. I was starting to learn to speak and read in English already.

The car came to a stop in a driveway next to a small, one-story wooden house with a small porch. It needed a fresh coat of paint. The lawn had bare spots. But there were flowers in the pots on the porch which reminded me of Hosteria San Luis. The house number was 613. I was at my new home.

CHAPTER TWENTY-FOUR

LIFE IN TOLEDO AND A THIRD NAME

From that moment on, Jerry became a real chatterbox. He spoke English really well and wanted me to learn quickly. Oma Jette still preferred to speak in German, but she tried to speak as much English as she could with me. I think she learned a lot more English during the time I lived in her house!

Jerry went around the house and put pieces of paper with the English word on every item in it: chair, radio, stove, table, can, fork, bed. You name it. I couldn't eat anything unless I said the word for it in English! The only bad part was that Jerry had a pretty heavy German accent and so I pronounced my first words just like him...until I started school.

There weren't many kids on Vermont Street. Most of the people living there were old, and many were old Jews originally from Europe. Of the few children, most were younger than me and all of them were black. I'd seen a few black people in Ecuador, mostly from the Chota Valley, when they came into Quito to sell things on market days. I certainly never lived or went to school with them.

That was a big change for me when I became enrolled in Sherman School. Since I was in the sixth grade in Ecuador, Jerry went with me on the first day of school to enroll me in the same grade. He explained to the principal that I was from Ecuador and didn't speak English. I think that's what he said. I still didn't understand English yet.

Jerry left and the principal gestured for me to follow her. The school was old and needed a fresh coat of paint. The ceilings were high. But we passed a large gymnasium and I could see a big playground, like the one at Colegio Americano, out a hallway window. I liked that. I wanted to get back to soccer right away.

The principal took me into a classroom filled with kids about my age. He talked to the teacher for a few minutes and left me. The teacher was a black woman! I couldn't believe it! And then I looked at the students in the classroom. About half of them were black, too. This sure wasn't Escuela Municipal Espejo.

The teacher pointed at herself and said, "Mrs. Carter." I nodded and repeated her name.

She pointed at me with a questioning look in her eye. "Enrique," I said, nodding. I turned to the class and pointed at myself, "Enrique."

Mrs. Carter shook her head. She wanted me to have an American name. Enrique is Spanish for Henry. There already was a boy named Henry in the class, I learned later. She shook her head, pointed at me and said, "Hank!"

I had a hard time pronouncing the "h." After a couple tries, it finally came out right.

"Hank!" I said proudly. The class said it after me.

And so I became Hank Cohen as long as I was in America.

School was only a half-day for the first day of classes. Oma Jette was at the school door as I came out, with a bag lunch. We sat on a bench near the playground to eat our sandwiches. It was a strange sandwich on a round sort of roll with an orangey-fishy filling and a smooth, white cheese: Bagel, lox, cream cheese. I liked it.

After lunch, we boarded a bus. It was nicer than the buses in Quito, with cushioned seats. The streets became wider and busier with all kinds of people dressed very nicely. There wasn't a single donkey like the ones I was used to seeing in Quito, carrying loads for their Indian owners. Where were the Indians I'd seen the American movies I'd seen with Augusto?

The buildings became taller the farther we went on the bus. Many were much taller than any I'd seen in Quito. The bus stopped in front of a tall building with a sign over the door "Medical Arts" where Oma Jette and I got off. I knew from the word "Medical" that we were going to see a doctor there about my boils. I was excited. Would I finally be cured?

145

We entered into a beautiful lobby, like I'd never seen before: a tall ceiling and floors made of different kinds of colorful marble stone. We waited for an elevator. I'd never been in one before and this was very exciting! The elevator opened to a long hallway with doors on each side and a marble floor like the one in the lobby. THIS was America!

We opened the door that said: Dr. Herbert Rothbart, Dermatology. The waiting room was luxurious to my eyes, too. There was beautiful carpeting, richly upholstered chairs, and the receptionist sat behind a counter with a marble top. Oma spoke slowly in English to the receptionist and I heard her say my name: Enrique Cohen, and then we sat down to wait.

In just a few minutes, a blonde woman in a crisp, white nurse's uniform opened a door and called "Cohen!" I thought to myself that she probably didn't want to try to pronounce "Enrique." Having a new, American name like Hank was a good idea.

We went an examination room that was a lot like the one at Dr. Sotomayor's clinic. In a minute, Dr. Rothbart came in. He greeted Oma in German and reached out to shake my hand. He was a tall, husky man with white hair rimming a bald head, and had a happy smile on his lips.

Oma Jette reached into her purse and pulled out a letter that I could see had been written by Mami. It was a long letter and Dr. Rothbart took a long time reading it, stopping now and then to say something to Oma Jette. Then he turned to me and gestured for me to remove my shirt and undershirt. I was anxious to show him my back and for him to cure me.

Dr. Rothbart looked, and touched, and poked my back, shaking his head occasionally when he spoke to Oma Jette. Finally, he turned to me, gave me a "thumbs up" and handed me my clothes. Again, he turned to Oma Jette, talked to her for a long time and then wrote something on a small pad of paper and gave it to her. I figured it was another prescription. Oma Jette seemed to thank him and shook both of his hands in hers. I said, "Gracias, Doctor Rothbart!" He was quite surprised to hear me speak and laughed. Then he shook my hand again. Like people do in Ecuador.

There was a pharmacy on the ground floor of the Medical Arts Building. We stopped there to fill the prescription and headed back to the house on Vermont Street on a bus.

That night was the start of a routine that lasted for several months. Every night before bed, I soaked in a warm tub with some sort of powder than Oma Jette stirred into it before I stepped in. Then, she put the prescription cream on my back. The first cream didn't do much good. We went back to Dr. Rothbart and tried a different prescription. It didn't do much good, either. The third time, we tried a different product, an oil, and that did the trick! I'm still using that oil and the boils haven't come back.

School was a different story. Most of the kids in my sixth grade class had been together since kindergarten. The black kids stuck together, though. The white kids had their groups. They both made fun of me because my English was bad. I was working really, really hard to catch up. I didn't want to fall behind in school. Mrs. Carter was terrific. She stayed after school with me whenever I asked to help me with reading and writing. I'll never forget her.

The one place where everyone mixed was on the baseball diamond. I was disappointed that no one knew about soccer, which is called football in Spanish. When I asked if anyone wanted to play football, they brought out this strange, brown, oval ball and tossed it between each other. I didn't know that the English word was soccer until I was ready to go home, many months after I started school. I was terrible at baseball. The skills you need for it are completely different from soccer skills. Sometimes they let me play center field because the ball seldom went in that direction.

In the end, I really didn't have a lot of time to play anything, even after I spoke English well.

My twelfth birthday happened shortly after I arrived in Toledo. A couple months later, Jerry asked me if I planned to be Bar Mitzvah. I'd heard those words mentioned by the Jewish kids at Colegio Americano. I knew it was some sort of Jewish ceremony for boys when they were thirteen years old. I always meant to ask Opa Max about it, but somehow never got around to it.

"Well, maybe," I told Jerry. "But I really don't know what's involved? What do I have to do?"

Jerry shook his head and murmured to himself, "Goyische kopf! Let's go to shul on Saturday. I think there's a bar mitzvah this week and you can see for yourself."

Shul. I'd heard my parents say that word a few times, but I never asked what it was. Just another German word I didn't know.

"Shul?" I asked.

"Gevalt!" Jerry exclaimed. "He doesn't know from shul! It's a synagogue! A place where Jews go to pray."

"Oh, a synagogue. I know what that is. It's almost the same in Spanish: sinagoga. I've just never been to one. I don't think we live near the one in Quito."

My English was improving — fast!

Jerry perked up. "It's a date!"

Saturday couldn't come fast enough. Jerry dressed up in a suit, but Oma Jette didn't want to join us. I wore a clean white shirt and one of Jerry's ties. We drove quite a distance before we came to a two-story building with pillars in front and a dome with a Jewish star on top of it. Letters in Hebrew were carved over the door and in English the words "Temple Shomer Emunim" were carved.

"I thought we were going to a synagogue," I said to Jerry. "This is a Temple!"

Jerry laughed and shook his head. "This is a Reform synagogue. Most of them are called temples around here."

I didn't know that there were different kinds of synagogues, but I was learning quickly.

We entered through a pair of large metal doors with what I assumed were Jewish symbols on them. There was a marble-floored lobby where people were greeting each other, mostly in a language that sounded a lot like German. Another set of large, carved wooden doors opened and I almost lost my breath! The room was beautiful with warm wood walls, tall windows, blue carpeting and blue upholstery on the chairs – like a movie theater! Only instead of a screen, at the front was some sort of cabinet and near the ceiling I could see the pipes of an organ, like I'd seen in some of the churches in Quito.

I decided I'd just watch and listen and not ask too many questions. It was all confusing, but beautiful at the same time. Finally, the rabbi (Jerry pointed him out to me) called a boy to the front of the stage and asked him to read from the Torah (Jerry told me about that, too). He was the Bar Mitzvah boy. He read a bit from the Torah and later gave a speech. I figured I might like to do that, too. Then came the best part: we went downstairs into a huge room where there were all kinds of great cookies and pieces of cake to eat. I *knew* I wanted to do that, too, if it was part of having a Bar Mitzvah!

As we drove home, Jerry asked me, "So, do you think you want to become a Bar Mitzvah?"

I didn't hesitate, "Yes, sir!"

"Then, next week I will talk to the rabbi and we will find you a tutor to prepare you."

"How long should it take?"

"Several months. But your birthday isn't until September. There's plenty of time!"

And so, three days a week after classes at Sherman School I took a bus to Shomer Emunim and sat with old Mr. Glaser who taught me what I needed to know to read my part of the Torah on my Bar Mitzvah day. Mr. Glaser was from Hungary and had been in a Nazi concentration camp. I could tell that because he had numbers tattooed on his arm like Oma Jette and Jerry did. Oma Jette and Jerry would not talk about the camp, so I never asked Mr. Glaser about it either.

The boils came back now and then, but not too badly. We knew that the hot baths helped.

One day Jerry said to me, "I'm going to the shvitz. Do you want to come with me? I think it will be good for your back. It's hot and steamy there, like that place you told me about in Ecuador. What did you call it?"

"Baños," I told him for the umpteenth time. I had no idea of what the shvitz was, but if it was anything like Baños right there in Toledo, I was ready for it! "Yes, let's go."

I was wrong.

The shvitz was an old building, nothing like the beautiful gardens and pool at Hosteria San Luis. It was a "Turkish steam bath." We walked into a room with lots of lockers and benches. There were a bunch of old men there, all friends of Jerry's. Most of them were naked already and were walking around with towels slung over their shoulders. I was horrified by what I saw. I'd never seen so many naked people together in my life. And these friends of Jerry's – there was something different about them below the waist that was different than what I had there. All of a sudden, I became very modest.

"Come on, Hank!" Jerry shouted. He liked to call me by my American name. "Don't be shy! We've all got the same equipment!" But we didn't.

The men started tickling me to force me to take off my undershorts. I had no choice. I stripped. The tickling stopped and so did their laughter. No one said anything more. We tied towels around our waists and filed into the steam room. Like Jerry said, it was good for my back. But it wasn't good for my pride.

Driving home in the car, Jerry asked me, "So what's with your peepee?"

I blushed. "It's always been this way."

"Didn't your parents have you circumcised when you were a baby, like all Jewish boys?"

"Cir-cum-cised?" It was a new English word for me. "You mean, make it look like all the men in the shvitz?'

He nodded, keeping his eyes on the road. This was as embarrassing for him as it was for me.

"Evidently not," I said softly. "But it's not *my* fault. I was a baby. You need to ask my parents."

"Well, that's not an easy thing to do, with how slow the mail is sometimes," he said. "But you can't become a Bar Mitzvah the way you are now. You're not totally a Jewish man. You saw me. You saw the others at the shvitz!"

"Does it hurt?"

"How do I know? I was eight days old!"

I thought about it. I wanted to have a Bar Mitzvah. I wanted to be a real Jewish man like Papi and Opa Max and Jerry. I didn't have any choice.

"Okay, I'll do it."

Jerry called the rabbi at Temple Shomer Emunim and asked him who could perform the "bris." I was learning Hebrew words now, too.

Thanksgiving was the next time I'd have a couple days off from school. We had an early Thanksgiving meal with friends of Jerry and Oma Jette. There were no children and everyone was speaking what I had learned by then was Yiddish. Though the food was good, I was glad to leave. Oma Jette, Jerry and I drove straight from the Thanksgiving feast to a small hospital not far from Temple Shomer Emunim that had a sign "The Jewish Hospital." Oma Jette hugged me as I was tucked into a hospital bed in the children's ward.

"Jerry will be with you in the morning," she said. "And so will Rabbi Segal from Shomer Emunim. Be brave!"

Those last words didn't help to make me feel brave.

I read a little. I walked over to a lounge where there was a television set. I'd never seen television before. It helped to take my mind off of what would happen to me the next morning. Would I feel differently, too – more Jewish – when there was a change in my body?

I don't remember the name of the doctor who performed the operation. He looked like some of the men at the shvitz. He looked Jewish. As promised, Jerry was there bright and early. And so was the rabbi. I'd met him a couple times when I went to meet with Mr. Glaser at Temple Shomer Emunim. They put me on a cart and wheeled me into an operating room. It was cold and all I was wearing was a hospital gown. I was shaking all over from the cold, nervousness, and excitement. Rabbi Segal said some stuff in Hebrew. Jerry and the doctor said "Amen." Then, they put the mask on me and the ether gas put me to sleep.

When I first woke up, nothing hurt. Jerry was sitting in a chair beside my bed. I had a drink of water, I think. I fell asleep again. It was after lunch when I awoke fully. I was hungry. And I hurt. You know where. A nurse came in and gave me a pill that made me feel better, but it also made me sleepy.

I slept again until dinner time. I was really hungry and I really hurt. You know where. But my hunger was bad enough that I stayed awake to eat what seemed like a sad imitation of the turkey dinner I'd eaten the day before. Jerry was gone. The nurse gave me another pill. I slept again.

Finally, the next morning, both Jerry and Oma Jette were there. She had made cookies for me. The cookies did almost as much to make me feel better as the pills did. I got out of bed to go to the bathroom. Wow! It hurt!

The doctor came to take a look at me and smiled when he unwrapped the bandage, and then put on a clean one.

"A beautiful job!" he congratulated himself. "The next time you go to the shvitz with your grandfather, the guys will think you had it done as a baby! Just keep it clean and the pain will go away in a couple days."

Before I could tell him that Jerry wasn't my grandfather, he'd turned on his heel and walked away. I thought to myself, maybe he was right. Jerry sure was acting like an Opa to me. I wondered if he had a family like Oma Jette and that they, too, died in the concentration camp like most of Papi's family. Maybe that's why he was treating me like his own grandson.

I went home with Oma Jette and Jerry that evening. The little wood house with the peeling paint on Vermont Street never looked so good to me before! But it wasn't home. It wasn't Quito Colonial with Mami, Papi, Opa Max and Oma Selma.

The following Friday night, Oma Jette took out two brass candlesticks and lit candles. She said to me in her German-accented English, "You are now a real Jew. I am supposed to light candles on Shabbos because I am the woman of the house. But tonight, I want *you* to light them. I will say the blessing."

Oma Jette had never lit Sabbath candles as long as I'd been there. She made a nice dinner and bought a challah on Friday night, but lighting candles was never were in the picture. Maybe it brought back too many sad memories of before the concentration camp.

I lit the candles and Oma Jette sang a blessing in Hebrew. It was a wonderful moment for me. It was the first time I felt truly Jewish.

CHAPTER TWENTY-FIVE

RETURN TO ECUADOR AND A FOURTH NAME

I arrived in Toledo in September of 1949, just before my twelfth birthday. I started Sherman School immediately. I learned to speak English like a real American there, with all the dirty words and slang expressions. And I learned math, and science, and history. But it was American history. No one was interested when I tried to tell a little about Ecuadorian history.

It was in late October that I started studying for my bar mitzvah. Mr. Glaser said I was probably his best student ever. He thought it was because I already spoke Spanish and was learning English quickly. I missed speaking Spanish.

I was amazed when winter came to Toledo. The snow fell fast and deep in the middle of December. I'd only seen snow on the top of the volcanoes of the Andes between Riobamba and Quito. It was great. It was one of the few times that the boys at school included me in their games, which mostly involved building snow forts and having snowball fights.

When the snow melted for good in March, the fun went with it.

My boils were gone. We knew how to keep them from coming back: warm water and air, and that prescription oil.

There really wasn't a good reason for me to stay in Toledo once the school year ended.

I got a letter from Mami in June, just as school was ending. It was in Spanish.

24 May, 1950
Quito

Dear Enrique,

All of us in Quito are fine and hope that you, your Oma Yette and Jerry are in the best of health and enjoying the springtime. I remember spring as a wonderful time in Tauhaubischelstein with different flowers coming into bloom every few days.

We miss you very much. Augusto Maldonado comes to the store every Friday to see if a letter has arrived from you. He has grown quite tall this past year. He will be going to a new school when the school year begins, Alliance Academy. They teach school on the American model there, in English, and he wants you to be in his class there when you come home.

I know that you have been preparing for bar mitzvah at Temple Shomer Emunim. Do you think you will want to have your ceremony there? I'm sorry to say that if you do, we will not be able to share the happiness of the day with you. But we will be content with whatever you decide. Quito's Jewish community started building a real synagogue here shortly after you left and it is almost completed now. It is near the new campus of the Central University, close to the Ejido Park.

Your Oma Jette wrote to tell me that your boils are gone and that we now know the best way to treat you if they ever return. That was the main reason we sent you to Toledo, to get you cured de una vez! If you want to stay in Toledo, we will understand. America is a land of riches. With Oma Jette there, you could easily become a citizen. But if you return to

Ecuador, the time has come when all of us here can become
Ecuadorian citizens.

Please write soon, once you have thought over what I
have written here, and tell us your decision.

Con todo carino de tu mami
Herta Sauer de Cohen

I read the letter twice. I'd never spent a summer in Toledo. But I really didn't have any friends my age to play with over the summer. Jerry worked for the Police Department. He had taken off a lot of time from work when I first came to Toledo and when I was in the hospital. Oma Jette liked staying in the house and she dressed like an old woman in shabby housedresses. She was so different from Oma Selma who was always doing something in the store and liked to dress well to make a good impression on our customers.

Oma Jette kept stationery, envelopes and stamps in a drawer in the kitchen. I went in and helped myself. I wrote to Mami in Spanish. It felt SO good! I told her that I wanted to come back to Quito as quickly as possible. That if they could afford to send me to Alliance Academy, I'd like to go. At least I knew I'd have one good friend to start out with there. I told her how thankful I was for them to pay for me to go to Toledo, using the last of the golden treasure that had helped our family through hard times for many years. I knew that there was a return ticket to Quito in the bag Mami had put around my neck at the Quito airport and that I was ready to use it.

I signed the letter "Con todo carino de tu hijo Enrique Cohen."

Oma Jette had been hanging clothes to dry on a rope line in the back yard. She came in and asked, "What does your mother write in the letter?"

"She wants me to decide if I want to stay in Toledo or go back to Ecuador."

"And what are you writing to her?"

I stopped for a minute. I didn't know if what I was going to tell Oma Jette would hurt her or be a relief to her.

"I'm telling her that I want to go back home to Quito."

I could see in a second that Oma Jette was happy. She broke out in a big smile and hugged me.

"We will miss you, but I will not take you away from your mama and papa forever like my other children were taken from me," she said. But she had a little tear in her eye.

On the last day of school, I said goodbye to my classmates. The next day I went to Temple Shomer Emunim for my last tutoring session with Mr. Glaser.

"I'm sorry I won't be able to hear you read your *haftarah*," he told me. "But I know you'll do a great job. Mazel tov in advance!"

The following Monday, Oma Jette took me for a last visit with Dr. Rothbart.

"Remember to keep your skin as moist as possible," he told me in English, without thinking that I might not understand everything he was saying. My English was very good now. "If you can go to – is it Baños? – or some place at sea level once or twice a year, it will help a lot. Keep using that prescription and you'll be fine!"

Every day, Oma Jette made another of my favorite Jewish foods that she usually only served on Shabbos. She was talking in English a lot more since I came and she told me some stories about my papi when he was my age. I could tell that she was afraid that I might forget her once I returned to Ecuador.

Jerry and I went to a travel agent on a Saturday and the agent arranged for my trip back to Quito. We sent a letter by air mail to Quito when we got home to tell Mami and Papi when to expect me at the airport.

The last Sunday before I was to return, Oma Jette, Jerry and I went on a wonderful trip together to Cedar Point in Sandusky, Ohio. I'd never been to an amusement park before. I rode three roller coasters there! I had never seen a lake as big as Lake Erie, either. Oma Jette, who seldom even smiled, was smiling and laughing as we rode on the merry-go-round. She said it reminded her of the carousel in Aurich when she was a child.

On the last day of June in 1950, we loaded up the car. Oma Jette had bought me another suitcase because she wanted to send gifts to everyone in our Quito family. We left Toledo in the late morning. I had a few tears in my eyes as the car drove away from the little wooden house on Vermont Street. It seemed to grow smaller and smaller as I looked out the car's back window. What had been so strange less than a year ago was now as dear to me as my family's house in Quito Colonial.

The drive though Ohio and Indiana was amazingly boring. I hadn't missed much on the night-time drive from Chicago to Toledo: flat land with miles after miles of corn growing in straight rows, broken up now and then by a farm house with a few cows or a tiny town with corn silos near a railroad track. Things changed when we got to Gary, Indiana with its huge steel mills belching smoke.

Chicago's airport looked familiar and we found the Panagra Airlines counter with no problems. I showed my ticket and passport to the agent.

"I'm going home to Quito!" I proclaimed.

"I see you're from Ecuador," the agent commented, "But you don't seem to have an accent. Your English is perfect."

I was bursting with pride and I could see that Oma Jette and Jerry stood up a bit taller when they heard the agent's compliment.

"Yes," I've been living with my grandparents in Toledo for the school year. I'm practically a gringo now!" I laughed inside myself, remembering how the man in Baños had called Mami and me gringos.

When we reached the departure gate, there were just a few minutes before I had to board the plane.

"Oma Jette," I said to her, "you have been so kind to me. Do not forget me, please. May God reward you."

She started crying. I turned to her husband and said, "Opa Jerry. You have been a wonderful friend and just like a real Opa to me. I will think of you when I stand before the Torah for my bar mitzvah and ask God's blessing on you."

He started crying. I started crying.

The stewardess came over and grabbed me by the shoulder.

"It's time to get on the plane," she said in English. Ten months ago, I wouldn't have understood a word she said. I nodded. I hugged Oma Jette and Opa Jerry, and then ran onto the plane so that I could turn my head to the window and cry without anyone seeing it. Would I ever see them again?

The plane went south, following the same route I'd taken north the year before. I had a book to read in English this time. I didn't need anyone special to guide me through the airport in Dallas to change planes. I could read all the signs. In some ways, I realized I was a different person now: older and more experienced in different languages and cultures.

I slept most of the way from Dallas to Quito. The pilot's voice woke me when he announced, "We are about to land in Quito at Mariscal Sucre Airport. If you look out the windows on the left, you will see the Cotopaxi volcano as we make our approach." I was on the left. It was the same incredibly clear and sunny kind of morning as it was on the day I left.

As I walked down the stairway, I saw a crowd of people pressed up against a chain-link fence next to the terminal. Everyone was waving at passengers as we stepped off the plane. And right in front were Mami, Papi, Opa Max, Oma Selma — and Augusto! But my first thought was: Who's watching the store? I couldn't wait to grab my suitcases and clear customs and immigration. The agent at the immigration desk looked at my passport and said, "Welcome back to Ecuador!" Those wonderful words were like music to my ears.

I had barely opened the doors to the street when I was enveloped with hugs by all of my family. Everyone was talking so fast in Spanish. I realized that I was having a hard time understanding them. It had been so long since I'd heard people speaking that way.

"Bienvenido! Bienvenido!" rang in my ears.

I had to twist my tongue to answer them quickly in Spanish, "Gracias! Que gusto de verles!" I was glad to see them.

Papi grabbed the door of a big taxicab and we all piled in. To me, the sights, sounds and smells of Quito seemed familiar yet different. I let others do the talking as I took it all in while we headed south toward Quito Colonial and our house. Everything seemed so cramped together. I had become used to the wide horizons of the Ohio landscape. We stopped at Nuevo Mercado Aleman to drop off Papi and Oma. It looked small and dark. I had gone to the modern supermarket in Toledo with Oma Jette many times, with its brightly-lit, wide aisles and endless choices of different kinds of food.

On the sidewalk next to the store was an old, sad, dirty Indian, begging for a coin or a piece of food. That beggar had sat in that same spot for years and years. I had gotten so used to him that he had become invisible to me. Now, I couldn't avoid seeing him and I looked into his eyes for the first time. I dug into my pocket and took out an Ecuadorian coin I'd carried with me all through my time in Toledo. I gave it to him.

"Dios le pague," he said to me, clasping my hand in gratitude. I don't recall ever seeing a beggar in Toledo.

Our house, too, was not as I remembered it. The patio was smaller and the plaster on the walls surrounding it was chipping off. I'd never noticed that before. My little bedroom seemed smaller and darker than ever. My room in the Vermont Street house had a big window that looked out onto the sunny back yard.

We had a light breakfast with our family's bread that I'd craved in Toledo. At lunch, we had all kinds of Ecuadorian food: a shrimp cebiche with slices of avocado, potato soup with cheese. For dessert, we had my favorite: quimobolitos, sweet dough wrapped in a cana leaf and boiled. Ahhhh!

I opened a suitcase and gave everyone the little gifts I'd bought and the bigger gifts from Oma Jette and Opa Jerry. I gave a gift to Augusto, too: a pennant from the Toledo Mudhens baseball team! I'd explain baseball to him later. Before I left, Opa Jerry had taken me to a game.

"You can't be a REAL American until you've been to a baseball game!" Jerry told me, laughing as he liked to do so much.

CHAPTER TWENTY-SIX

THE BOY GETS HIS FOURTH NAME

In no time, life returned to what it had always been. I went back to Escuela Municipal Especial with Augusto. School had ended in Toledo, but it still was in session in Quito. Augusto told me that we wouldn't have much of a vacation when the school year ended because in a few weeks, we'd be starting at Alliance Academy. It followed the school year in the United States.

That was fine with me. I found the schoolwork easy compared to what we did at Sherman School. I finished my homework in no time. That gave me more chance to continue practicing my *haftarah* for my bar mitzvah. I didn't want to forget it. On Sundays, Papi would sit and listen to me as I read the words with the sing-song chant.

My thirteenth birthday would be just a couple weeks after the start of school at Alliance Academy. I don't know which excited me more: going to a new, American-style school or the idea of standing in front of the Jewish community for my bar mitzvah, as I'd seen at Shomer Emunim in Toledo. At Alliance Academy, most of the kids were Americans and I told them to call me Hank.

To prepare for my bar mitzvah, Mami took me to a tailor and I got a new suit. She bought a new dress, too, and a hat. I knew this must be very important for her to spend so much money for something that lasted for only one morning.

My birthday was September 19, and the Saturday after that was September 23, 1950. It was the day I was to become a Bar Mitzvah. I still didn't know much about Judaism. I didn't know about the holidays, except that there was a Seder on Passover. I didn't know the history of the Jews, except that we started out in Palestine (which had just become the State of Israel) and that everyone like Hitler and Mussolini hated us. I knew that Friday night was the Sabbath and that it was special. But I also knew that Jews stuck together and that we were special to God. I wanted to have people I could count on and I wanted to be special to God. I had gone through a bris so that I could become a Bar Mitzvah. It was time to do it.

That Saturday, Papi went to the synagogue before the rest of the family. The rest of us followed in a taxi. We drove north toward the airport, took a left at the Ejido Park instead of taking a right to go to Colegio Americano. In just a block or two, the taxi stopped in front of a building that clearly was still under construction. There was a tall wall in front with flowering vines growing over it, and a gate with a guard. The building looked like a very large house, and there was a sign over the front door, Beneficencia Israelita. It looked nothing like Shomer Emunim.

The guard opened the gate to us. We walked up the steps and entered. There was no marble floor, no beautifully-carved wooden doors. There was a sign by the front door: Today: Bar Mitzvah of Enrique Cohen. Yes, this was the place I was to become Bar Mitzvah.

We walked down a short hall. I could hear the voice of a man singing, but no organ. There was a cabinet with prayer shawls – I didn't know what it was at first, but Opa Max explained – and little caps that he and I wore. Before Mami and Oma turned to go up a stairway, Mami turned to me and said, "I know that you will make us all proud."

Where were they going? Opa and I walked through a set of doors. I almost turned around to walk out right then and there. This was nothing like Shomer Emunim. It was a very simple auditorium with an Ark for the Torah on one platform, and another platform was in front of it where a man stood, reading in a loud voice in Hebrew. He swayed back and forth as he chanted. Everyone was talking –or were they praying—without paying much attention to what the man was saying. I looked around. I spied Mami and Oma up in a balcony with a few other women. They waved to me. At Shomer Emunim, the women and men sat together and no one wore a prayer shawl or cap.

But everyone there was Jewish. I saw most of my soccer friends sitting with their fathers. I was surprised to see them. I hadn't played soccer with them for over a year now. But it proved, as Papi had told me, that Jews stick together and support each other. Elio Schaechter waved to me. I felt more at ease with my Italian-Ecuadorian-Jewish friend there. He had kept his Italian name, but I preferred my Ecuadorian name, Enrique, to the Italian Enrico that had been given to me at birth. There was no one there from Alliance Academy where I was called Hank, like in Toledo.

When they took the Torah out of the Ark, I knew my time was coming soon. Papi was given the honor of carrying the Torah around the auditorium. Then he sat in a seat on the platform.

One after another, different men were called up to bless the Torah and to hear part of it read. After a while, Opa gave me a nudge and took me by the hand up to where the Torah lay on a high table. The cantor sang quite a yodeling, loud announcement and then looked at me. He waited. I didn't know what he wanted from me.

"What's your Hebrew name?" he asked.

"Enrico?"

"That's not Hebrew!" the cantor snarled, then turned to Papi. "What's his Hebrew name?"

Papi rose and walked over to where we stood in front of the congregation.

"His name is Tzvi ben Avraham!" he declared. It was the first time I'd heard that name. But I knew it was mine and that I would become Tzvi ben Avraham every time I walked into a synagogue from then on.

With Papi and Opa Max on either side of me, I sang the blessing. When the cantor finished reading, I sang the other blessing. The words just came out of my throat and through my lips as if I had been saying them all my life.

Then I sang the blessing for the *haftarah*. Then I chanted the whole *haftarah*. I had memorized it so well that I didn't have to think about it. When I finished, a rumble came from the congregation. They were surprised and they were impressed! Who was this boy who had never been seen before at the Beneficencia Israelita who chanted the *haftarah* to perfection?

Shouts came up from their seats, "Mazel tov! Yasher koach!"

Opa Max hugged me. Papi shook my hand so hard that I thought it would fall off. He pounded my back hard, "Excellent work! We are proud!" I was really glad that I didn't have boils on my back any more.

When the Torah was returned to the Ark and everyone had taken their seats, the rabbi called me up to the platform.

"This is your time to speak to the congregation as a Bar Mitzvah," he said.

I stood looking at the crowd. I had not prepared a speech. Then I looked up at the balcony and saw Oma and Mami, smiling like never before. I had something to say to *them*.

"Good Shabbos," I started. Everyone who'd spoken before had started their comments with "good Shabbos", so I figured I should do it, too.

"I am proud to be here today. I have come a long way to be bar mitzvah," I stopped to think. I decided not to talk about my circumcision. "I want to thank people who helped me prepare, but who could not be here today. My Oma Jette and her husband, my Opa Jerry Oberlin, arranged for me to have lessons in Toledo, Ohio to learn the blessings and *haftarah*. Mr. Glaser was my tutor. He tried to explain the meaning of the words, but sometimes I didn't understand what he said in English, and he didn't speak any Spanish."

The congregation chuckled.

"I want to thank my grandparents Oma Selma and Opa Max Sauer, who always showed me love. I want to thank my parents, Herta and Abraham Cohen. They have made many sacrifices to make sure that I have good health. They make sure I'm getting a good education. Someday I want to go to the University of Michigan, which is near Toledo, Ohio, my American home. My parents ran from Hitler and Mussolini to make a better life for me here in Ecuador. Our life here keeps getting better. My life keeps getting better.

"Today I have become a man in the eyes of the Jewish community. I am learning who I am as a Jew. Today I got a new name, Tzvi ben Avraham. That says that I am a Jew. I was born Enrico. Many people call me Hank. And I always think of myself as Enrique. I am proud to be an Ecuadorian Jew and promise that I will always be loyal to the Jewish people and the country of Ecuador."

That's who I am.

AFTERWORD

At the time of this book's publication in 2021, the real Enrique Cohen was alive and well and living in Quito. Enrique graduated from the University of Michigan and met his wife, Gail Hochman, there. They've made their life together in Quito. Their two children live in the United States, as do their grandchildren, but have maintained strong ties to Ecuador.

The Cohen-Sauer family members were successful in several businesses in the Quito area, and for a while owned an hacienda on the upper elevations of Mt. Cayambe where they raised dairy cattle. Enrique became a businessman who literally helped to expand the growth of Quito in the 1970s-90s with his brick factory. Other Jews played prominent roles in the development of Quito and Ecuador in the twentieth century:

Alberto Di Capua Ascoli and Carlos Alberto Ottolenghi from Italy were among the founders of LIFE Pharmaceutical Laboratories in Quito, one of the largest in South America.

Kurt Dorfzaun, a refugee from Germany in Cuenca, expanded the production of "Panama" hats, making them more accessible and affordable to an international market.

Olga Fisch, a refugee from Hungary, founded a well-known fashion company and art gallery which combined fine art with typical motifs of traditional Ecuadorian design.

Karl Wilhelm (Carlos G.) Liebmann from Germany founded Ecuador's largest chain of bookstores "Su Libreria" and professionalized book selling in the country.

Benno Weiser from Austria became the first columnist in an Ecuadorian newspaper and subsequently was a key player in the foundation of the country's first television station.

GLOSSARY

WORD IN TEXT	TRANSLATION	LANGUAGE SOURCE
Abuelita	Grandma	Spanish
Adios	Goodbye	Spanish
Addio	Goodbye	Italian
Arti Liberali	Liberal Arts	Italian
Autocarril	Narrow-gauge railroad	Spanish
Avanti	Let's go	Italian
Bambino	Baby	Italian
Bar Mitzvah	Coming of age ceremony	Hebrew
Basta	Enough	Italian and Spanish
Bene	Good, well	Italian
Benvenuti	Welcome (to a group)	Italian
Bienvenidos	Welcome (to a group)	Spanish
Bitte	Please	German
Bris	Ritual circumcision	Hebrew/Yiddish
Buena suerte	Good luck	Spanish
Buona fortuna	Good luck	Italian
Buongiorno	Good morning/good day	Italian

Carino	Affection	Spanish
Challah	Braided bread loaf	Hebrew
Chuppah	Marriage canopy	Hebrew
Colegio	Upper School	Spanish
Danke schoen	Thank you	German
Diez de agosto	Tenth of august	Spanish
Dybbuk	Monster	Yiddish
Erev Shabbos	Friday night	Yiddish/Hebrew
Escuela	Elementary school	Spanish
Gevalt	Oh, my goodness	Yiddish
Goedemorgen	Good morning	Dutch
Goyische kopf	(an insult)	Yiddish
Grazie	Thank you	Italian
Guten abend	Good evening/hello	German
Guten tag	Good day/hello	German
Haftarah	A section the Bible	Hebrew
HaMotzi	Blessing over bread/grace	Hebrew
Hasta luego	See you later	Spanish
Hosteria	Resort hotel	Spanish
Jawohl	Yes	German
Jude	Jew/Jewish	German
Judio	Jew/Jewish	Spanish
Kaddish	Memorial prayer	Hebrew
Kugel	Baked pudding/loaf	Yiddish

Mach schnell	Hurry up!	German
Matzo	Unleavened bread for Passover	Hebrew
Mazel tov	Good luck/congratulations	Hebrew
Meine freunde	My friends	German
Meine liebe	My dear	German
Mezuzah	Ritual container for scripture	Hebrew
Mikveh	Ritual bath	Yiddish
Minyan	Quorum for group prayer	Hebrew
Mohel	Person who performs a circumcision	Hebrew
Oma	Grandma	German
Opa	Grandpa	German
Ovviamente	Obviously	Italian
Rosh haShana	Jewish New Year	Hebrew
Seder	Festive meal at Passover	Hebrew
Shalom	Hello/Goodbye/Peace	Hebrew
Shomer Emunim	Guardian of the Faithful	Hebrew
Shul	Synagogue	Yiddish
Shvitz	Steam bath	Yiddish
Sinagoga	Synagogue	Spanish
Torah	Scroll of the 5 Books of Moses	Hebrew
Wellkomen	Welcome	Dutch
Yasher Koach	Well done!	Hebrew
Yiddish	Common language of Eastern European Jews	Yiddish

BIBLIOGRAPHY

The Halo of the Jungle, Gert and Werner Aron, Aron Publications, 1999.

La Migracion Judia en Ecuador: Ciencica, cultura y exilio 1933-1945, Academia Nacional de Historia, 2018.

Ahora que Cae la Niebla, Oscar Vela, Alfaguara (Penguin Random House Grupo Editorial), 2019.

Interviews that helped to create the events in the story:

Eva Balcazar
Enrique Cohen
Catalina Cohn
Lilli Cohn
Michael Desrosier
Walter Karger
Herbert Max
Siegfried Rosenthal
Elio Schachter
Boris Suster

Made in the USA
Monee, IL
10 September 2021